Praise for Cynthia Ozick and

Dictation

"There are many reasons to admire Cynthia Ozick's fiction —stylistic verve, sly humor, kindliness, engagement with serious themes . . . *Dictation* shows that Ozick continues to command her usual mastery of voices and tones . . . it'll be hard to stop reading once you start."— *Washington Post Book World*

"Such delicious mischief . . . as rich and entertaining as a high-comic novel."— *Boston Globe*

"Cynthia Ozick is double-barreled. She's an inventive and revelatory fiction writer and an exacting, battle-ready critic; an impish writer of conscience and a creative intellectual."
— *Los Angeles Times Book Review*

"A sly and witty exploration of literary style and immortality . . . All four stories in this captivating collection explore what it means to dissimulate and deceive—and the importance of being, not earnest, but playful."— *Christian Science Monitor*

"Vividly imaginative . . . *Dictation* is a charming book."
— *St. Louis Post-Dispatch*

"Ozick's expert ventriloquism, her gift for the rhythms and idiosyncrasies of speech, stands out on every page. She breathes fire into her characters and makes them easy to love, as much for their deceptions as for their virtues."
— *Charleston Post and Courier*

Dictation

BOOKS BY CYNTHIA OZICK

NONFICTION

Quarrel & Quandary
Fame & Folly
Metaphor & Memory
Art & Ardor
The Din in the Head

FICTION

Dictation
Heir to the Glimmering World
The Puttermesser Papers
The Shawl
The Messiah of Stockholm
The Cannibal Galaxy
Levitation: Five Fictions
Bloodshed and Three Novellas
The Pagan Rabbi and Other Stories
Trust

DICTATION

A Quartet

CYNTHIA OZICK

MARINER BOOKS
HOUGHTON MIFFLIN HARCOURT
Boston • New York

First Mariner Books edition 2009

www.hmhbooks.com

Library of Congress Cataloging-in-Publication Data
Ozick, Cynthia.
Dictation : a quartet / Cynthia Ozick.
p. cm.
ISBN 978-0-547-05400-1
ISBN 978-0-547-23787-9 (pbk.)
I. Title.
PS3565.Z5D53 2008
813'.54—dc22   2007052331

Book design by Melissa Lotfy

Printed in the United States of America

DOC 10 9 8 7 6 5 4 3 2 1

"Actors" and "At Fumicaro" were previously published
in *The New Yorker*. "What Happened to the Baby?"
first appeared in the *Atlantic Monthly*.

To
D.M. and M.J.,
life changers

MY HAPPIEST THANKS ARE OWED TO
DAVID MILLER, WHO SAW THE FOX.

Contents

DICTATION

In the early summer of 1901, Lamb House, Henry James's exurban domicile in Rye, was crowded with flowers. At the close of the morning's dictation, Mary Weld, his young amanuensis, had gone out to the back garden with scissors in hand, to cut the thorny vines that clung to the heat of a surrounding brick wall. On the entrance hall table, on the parlor mantelpiece, on the dining room sideboard — everywhere in the house where the eyes of the expected visitors might fall — she scattered rose-filled vases. Then she mounted her bicycle and rode off.

The visitors did not arrive until late afternoon. Tea was already laid, as usual with safe and respectable toast and jam, but also with the perilously sweet and oily pastries James was so fond of, though they made his teeth hurt horribly. Even before the knocker was lifted, he knew they had come: here were the wheels of the trap scraping on gravel, and the pony's skipping gait, and a child's angry howl when he was taken from his mother and set down before an alien door. James stood waiting, nervously braiding his fingers — Lamb House was unaccustomed to the presence of a noisy, unpredictable, and certainly precarious three-year-old boy, and one with so un-English a name.

Four years before, James had summoned Joseph Conrad to lunch at 34 DeVere Gardens, his London flat. The two of them sat in the unsteady yellow light of newly installed electric bulbs and talked of the nature of fiction — yet not quite as writer to writer. Conrad was a stringy, leathery, youthful-looking man of nearly forty, a literary cipher, virtually unknown. As an act of homage, he had sent James a copy of *Almayer's Folly,* his first — at that time his only — novel. James saw something extraordinary in it, even beyond the robustness of style and subject: he saw shrewdness, he saw fervency, he saw intuition, he saw authority; he saw, in rougher circumstance, humanity. In a way, he saw a psychological simulacrum of himself — and in a Polish seaman!

Awed and self-conscious, Conrad could scarcely lick away the grains of crumpet lingering on his lower lip. He understood himself to be a novice still, perpetually distraught and uncertain: was his stuff any good at all? And he worried, in these rooms of high privilege, and under the false yellow light with its unholy flicker, whether his pronunciation was passable. Sometimes he used words, marvelous English words, that he had only *read,* and when he spoke the marvelous words, no matter how intimately he felt them, their syllables, striking the surprised eyes of his hearers, seemed all in the wrong tones: he could not bring out, except in ink, that sublimely organized Anglo-Saxon speech. Polish was otherwise constructed; now and then he borrowed the counterpoint of its ornate melodies, but he would never again write in his native language. He would not — he could not — speak to his wife in any foreign voice; she knew no language other than her own. Despite what was called a "natural" intelligence, she had little education. She was sensible and good-hearted and straightforward and comfortably dependable. He harbored some small shame over her, and was ashamed of his shame. He hid it, as much as he could, even from himself. He had learned, early on, the difference between common sense and infatuation; marriage meant the former. In this initial colloquy with the Master (he hoped others would follow), he was reluctant to disclose that he was, in fact, a new husband, and that he had only recently, and willingly, thrown himself into the coils of domesticity. There was nothing in his wife's character to attract James's always inquisitive ear — was this why he was blotting out his Jessie? Or was it because James, in all the nobility of his supreme dedication, led an unencumbered bachelor life, altogether freed to his calling? While a man with a wife, and perhaps soon with a child . . .

DeVere Gardens had saluted the coming century — the nascent twentieth — with artificial illumination, and also with an innovation growing more and more commonplace. It was said that the Queen had requested the new thing for her secretary, who had refused it in terror. On a broad surface reserved for it in a far corner of the room where the older writer sat discoursing, and the younger went on nodding his chin with an affirmative and freshly inaugurated little pointed beard, stood the Machine. It stood headless and armless and legless — brute shoulders merely: it might as well have been the torso of a broken god. Even at a distance it struck Conrad as strange and repulsive, the totem of a foreign civilization to which, it now appeared, James had uncannily acclimated. The thing was large and black and glossy, and in height it ascended in tiers, like a stadium. Each round key was shielded by glass and rimmed by a ring of metal. James had been compelled to introduce the Machine into his labors after years of sweeping a wrist across paper; gripping a pen had become too pain-

ful. To relieve the recurring cramp, he hired William Mac-
Alpine, a stenographer, who recorded in shorthand James's
dictation and then transcribed it on the Machine; but it soon
turned out to be more efficient to speak directly to the thing
itself, with MacAlpine at the keys.

Their glassy surfaces were catching the overhead light.
Shifting his head, Conrad saw blinking semaphores.

"I note, sir," James remarked, "that you observe with some
curiosity the recent advent of a monstrously clacking but oh so
monumentally modern Remington. The difficulty of the matter is that my diligent typewriter, a plausible Scot conveniently
reticent, is at bottom too damnably expensive, and I believe I
can get a highly competent little woman for half, *n'est-çe pas?*
May I presume, Mr. Conrad, that you, in the vigor of youth, as
it were, are not of a mind to succumb to a mechanical interces-
sor, as I, heavier with years, perforce have succumbed?"

Dictation? Dependence? Inconceivable separation of hand
from paper, inner voice leaching into outer, immemorial sacred solitude shattered by a breathing creature always in sight,
a tenacious go-between, a constantly vibrating interloper, the
human operator! The awful surrender of the fructuous mind
that lives on paper, lives *for* paper, paper and ink and nothing else! Squinting upward at the electrical sorcery suspended
from the ceiling, a thread of burning wire that mimicked and
captured in its tininess the power of fire, it occurred to Conrad that Jessie at her sewing might covet this futuristic advan-
tage. As for himself and the Machine ... never. He had his
seaman's good right hand, and the firm mast of his pen, and
the blessèd ocean of paper, as white as a sail and as relentless
as the wind.

"An amanuensis?" he replied. "No, Mr. James, I am not so
progressive. Indeed I loathe revolution. I have run steam in

my day, but I was trained to the age of sail. I fear I am wed-
ded to my bad old habits."

⚮

Not long after Conrad's introduction to DeVere Gardens,
James gave up the implacable press and rush of London and
went to live in the country, in his cherished Lamb House — an
established householder at last. He took MacAlpine and the
Machine with him. But on this warm June afternoon in 1901,
when Conrad and Jessie and their son Borys came to visit,
changes were evident on both sides. For one, MacAlpine had
been replaced by the highly competent (and cheaper) little
woman James had hoped for: Miss Weld. And for another,
James now knew to a certainty that Conrad had a wife — a
plump wife made all the plumper by a plethora of bulging
and writhing bundles, among them the screeching child forc-
ibly lifted over the threshold, a multiform traveling nursery to
serve his exigencies, and a dangling basket of ripe plums. Her
tread was nevertheless light, though with a bit of a limp from
a knee injured in girlhood. The plums, she explained, were for
their host, not that the little boy wouldn't like two or three, if
Mr. James wouldn't mind, and would Mr. James please excuse
the child, he'd been dozing the whole eighteen miles from
Kent, it was the waking so abruptly when they arrived set him
off . . . She had the unschooled accent of the streets; her father had toiled in a warehouse.

Conrad, James saw, kept apart from wife and son, as if they
had been strangers who were for some unfathomable reason attaching themselves to his affairs. He was much altered
from the grateful young acolyte of DeVere Gardens. He carried himself with a look that hinted at a scarred and haughty
nature. He had since brought out half a dozen majestic works

7

of fiction; two of them, *The Nigger of the "Narcissus"* and *Lord Jim,* had already placed him as a literary force. He and James regularly exchanged fresh volumes as soon as they were out; each acknowledged the other as an artist possessed — though in private each man harbored his reservation and his doubt. James thought Conrad a thicket of unrestrained profusion. Conrad saw James as heartless alabaster. Writing, Conrad had confided, meant dipping his pen in his own blood and pulling out pieces of flesh. He was always despairing, and as a family man he was always in need of money. Very often he was ill. His nerves were panicked and untrustworthy. Those long-ago voyages in the tropics, Malaysia and Africa, had left him debilitated — the effects of malaria contracted in the Congo, and a persistent gout that frequently landed him in bed. The gout assaulted his joints; his writing hand was no good. There were times when it was agony to hold on to a pen. He had set Jessie to making fair copies of his big hurling hurting scrawl; she was eager and diligent, but when he looked over her neatly lettered sheets, he found foolish misreadings, preposterous omissions. She was not suited for the work. She was bright enough, she could compose an acceptable sentence on her own in decent everyday practical prose; she understood much of the ordinary world; she understood *him;* it was only that she lacked an eye for his lightning storms, his wild rushes and terrifying breathlessness. It grieved him that she was capable of converting a metaphor into a literalism (but this too was a metaphor), and she in her good plain way grieved that she could not satisfy his ferociously driven greed for the word, the marvelous English word. His handwriting was so difficult! But she had a cousin, she reminded him, a cousin who had gone to secretarial school; the cousin was properly trained, surely she would do better? The cousin was hired. She did not do better.

James was contemplating the child. That red elastic mouth with its tiny teeth, those merciless unstinting rising howls, was there to be no end to it? Was there a devil in this small being? And was this hellish clamor, and these unwanted plums with their sour skins, the common fruit of all marriage? Ah, the lesson in it!

"My dear Mrs. Conrad," he began in his most companionably embracing manner (the graciousness of mere twaddle, he liked privately to call it), "is it not possible that a simple bribe might induce calm in the breast of this vociferous infant? Here you are, my little man, a tart truly sublime upon the palate —"

Borys reached for the truly sublime stickiness and threw it in the air and resumed the rhythm of his protests: he wailed and he flailed, and Jessie said cheerily, with a glance at her stoically indifferent husband, "Oh do forgive us, Mr. James, but all these lovely bunches of roses ... then would there be a garden? Borys would love a romp in a garden, and this, you see, will permit you and Mr. Conrad to enjoy each other's company, would it not? I assure you that Borys and I will be very happy in the outdoors."

James did not hesitate. "Mrs. Smith," he called, "would you kindly oblige us —"

A servant materialized from a hidden corridor, bearing a large steaming iron kettle. A smell of spirits came with her.

"Sir, will you be wanting the hot water for the teapot now?"

"Not quite yet, Mrs. Smith. Mrs. Conrad and this very delightful young man will be pleased to be escorted to the floral precincts beyond the premises, and I beg you, Mrs. Smith, do take away that perilous object before we are all scalded to embers —"

Mrs. Smith looked confused, but Jessie picked up Borys

and followed her. The woman walked unsteadily, spilling boiling droplets. Mr. James, Jessie thought, was undoubtedly an
unearthly intelligence — had he actually uttered "floral precincts"? Still, she pitied him. He had no wife to run his house.
A wife would have a notion or two about what to do with a
drunken servant!

She did not know what the two men talked about that long
afternoon. As usual, she was shut out, though she thirsted
to hear. There was a cat in the garden, and Borys was sufficiently amused through the hours of exile. If only Mr. James
would come out to see how charming her little boy really
was! But Mrs. Smith had been directed to carry half the tea
things into the garden, where she set a table for Jessie and the
child. Plainly, it was Conrad who had maneuvered this ar-
rangement — or so Jessie believed. Her nostrils tightened: the
woman did smell awfully of whiskey, and her faltering steps
over the uneven ground made the tray of pastries wobble. One
of them dropped to the grass nearby, luring the cat, who gave it
a lick and left it alone. Soon a party of ants massed underfoot.
But except for the ants, and after a time a squad of circling
bees, it was pleasant in these secluded floral precincts (oh, that
remarkable man's way of speaking!); she had taken along her
sewing, and Borys was content to stalk the cat along the wall,
or to draw its silky tail through his fingers. Mrs. Smith, in a
second appearance, had inexplicably brought out the basket
of plums. Jessie was alarmed, and felt it an insult to their host,
when, looking up from her needle, she noticed that Borys had
eaten every last one. He had also consumed four of the sticky
tarts, and finally fell asleep in the late sun, with his head on
the cat.

When they had thanked Mr. James, and Jessie had apologized for the disappeared plums, and they had said their
goodbyes, and were halfway home in the trap, Jessie asked

Conrad what had been the chief points of the conversation indoors.

"Books," said Conrad. And then: "That damnable racket, what on earth was ailing the boy?"

"It was only he was hungry," Jessie said. "But what was Mr. James telling you?"

"You oughtn't to have brought the fruit. He doesn't like them raw."

"Is *that* what the two of you talked about?"

"Only in passing. Books mostly."

"His own? Yours?"

"Everybody's, so make an end of it, Jess. And we won't be taking the boy again, that's clear."

The plums had been mentioned, yes, but only because of the tarts — Mrs. Smith, tipsy as she regrettably too often was in her kitchen, had despite this impediment a knack, James said, for the manufacture of fruit pastries, which doubtless accounted for the size of his butter bill. From the cost of dairy, they passed on to writerly gossip — H. G. Wells was in the general neighborhood, at Sandgate on the coast, and Stephen Crane, the brilliant young American, at Brede, a mere eight-mile bicycle run to Rye; and also Ford Madox Hueffer, at Winchelsea. In fact, Hueffer had turned up only yesterday, bringing Edmund Gosse. So many intimate connections! In this very season, with an eye to the market, Conrad and Hueffer were collaborating on a novel, hoping to win the popular libraries — a thing that bemused James, since their separate styles had little in common. This observation led naturally to a discussion of style, and whether it remains distinct from the writer's intrinsic personality. Conrad thought not. The novelist, he argued (while out of the blue a shooting pain was assaulting his knuckles), surely the novelist stands confessed in his works? On the other hand, James countered (but the hurt just then was in both the poor visitor's hands: that cursèd gout flaring up when least desired!), the artist *multiplies* his confessions, thereby concealing his inmost self. The talk went back and forth in this way, the two labyrinthine minds locking and unlocking, and how, after all, was Conrad reasonably to recount it all to Jessie when she pressed him on it, as she was certain to do? James was free; there was no one to press him; yet Conrad was determined to press him now. As for style, he persisted, was there not an intervening influence, a contamination or a crippling, however you may tell it, when the roiling abyss, in whose bottommost bowel the secrets of language lie coiled, is thrown open to mundane elements? *Cher maître,* what of your Machine, your MacAlpines and Welds! Your sharers and intercessors!

It was past sundown when Conrad and Jessie reached their cramped old farmhouse—a property rented from Hueffer, and not far from Winchelsea, to facilitate the collaboration. After Borys had been put to bed, and Jessie had resumed her sewing, Conrad fell into his old complaint.

"It came on so, Jess, the pain in my hands, that I could hardly keep my wits. And worse in the right, as always."

"Oh my dear, and you haven't held a pen all day—"

"I had it from Mr. James that he has done well enough with his Remington these last years. I had rather thought it a vise, but he assures me that the whole of *The Ambassadors* was spoken aloud, and he believes it has enriched his tone—he feels his very breathing has gone into it. That glorious lavishness, dictated! And he finds Miss Weld decidedly a jewel. Jess, I have been too faint-hearted. Likely one can get one of these Remingtons at a fair price—Mr. James calculated for me the cost of his own. I'm confident we'll soon be able to afford it, especially if all goes right with Hueffer and the work."

Jessie let out a small snort. "The work," she said. "It appears to me it's you does most of it. It's not him that'll make your fortune. A man who won't keep his own name, and goes about calling himself Ford Ford, like a stutterer!"

"But you see," he held firm, "it's not to be just the cost of the Remington —"

"Of course I see. There's to be a Miss Weld. You want a jewel of your own." Her warming good humor came tumbling out in all its easy laughter. "Well, Mr. Conrad, this *will* be a revolution! And here you let me think the two of you were talking all afternoon about plums."

☙

Winter in Lamb House, when few visitors came, was lonely for Henry James; too often an insidious depression set in. At times he felt defined by it. It was, he admitted — especially to himself — deeper than anything else in his character, deeper even than the subterranean windings of his art. An extraordinary avowal: in the country he kept it hidden under great gusts of hospitality. But London, whatever its flaws, had never been openly lonely, and the Reform Club, where he took up seasonal residence in spacious upper rooms, and could entertain guests at luncheon in the pillared splendors below, was the metropolis at its finest. His windows oversaw the rooftops and chimney pots of handsome embassies and lofty mansions. It was here that he shaved off his whitening beard, itself a reason for melancholy: he thought it made him look old. And it was here, on a rainy afternoon in January of 1910, that Miss Lilian Hallowes and Miss Theodora Bosanquet almost did not meet.

Conrad and his wife had come to London to consult a surgeon. Jessie was suffering from the effects of her last knee operation (there had already been several), and would need yet another — some years earlier, she had fallen on the pavement during a shopping excursion, further damaging the troublesome injury of her teens. She had begun to take on the life of a serious cripple. Availing himself of an interval in the day's plans — Jessie was resting in their hotel — Conrad had arranged for Miss Hallowes to deliver some newly transcribed pages of his current work to the Reform Club, where James, learning his friend was in town, had invited him for one of their old talks. Conrad's instructions were plain: he had some necessary revisions in mind, and meant to apply them immediately. Miss Hallowes was to make herself known to the concierge, and was then simply to ascend to Mr. James's quarters, hand over the typewritten sheets to her employer, and rapidly and unobtrusively depart. Any chance of an encounter with Miss Bosanquet, however fleeting, must be urgently avoided. It was an hour when James would likely be dismissing Miss Bosanquet at the close of the morning's dictation. He was intermittently engaged at this time in composing the prefaces for his crowning New York Edition; his ambition was to gather up, and at last to perfect, all the novels and tales, the labors of a lifetime. He intended to vet each one, line by line, imposing his maturer style on his earlier manner, and he was looking forward to hearing Conrad's view of this obsessive revisiting — after so many years, did Conrad still hold to his theory that style confesses the inner man? And what if style were finally to be altered? Might it not signify that one's essential self, one's ostensibly immutable character, was, in fine, mutable?

When Conrad, considerably rain-dampened, penetrated the Grecian luxuriances of the Reform Club's lower halls, he had no inkling that this was to be the quizzical, possibly the fraught, theme of the visit. But he knew anyhow that the simultaneous appearance of the two ladies, in the presence of himself and James, would be damnably awkward. Miss

Hallowes had seen (was constantly seeing) into the blackest recesses of his mind. She was privy to his hesitations, his doubts, his reversals, and certainly his excitements; she was in the most crucial sense his double, since everything that came out of him she instantly duplicated on the Machine. His thoughts ran straight through her, unchanged, unmitigated, unloosed. Without doubt the same was true with respect to James and the spirited Miss Bosanquet: every vibration of James's sensibility ran through the woman who served and observed — how could it be otherwise? These two, Miss Hallowes and Miss Bosanquet, brought together even momentarily, could only mean exposure. In Miss Hallowes's face, in her posture, in the very shape and condition of her shoes, James would detect, with the divining rod that was his powerful instinct, the secret thing Conrad harbored against him: that the Master's cosmopolitanism, his civilized restraint, his perfection of method, his figures so finished, chiseled, and carved, were, when you came down to it, stone. Under the glow lay heartlessness and cold. And in Miss Bosanquet's face and posture and perhaps even in the shape and condition of her shoes, Conrad himself might recognize, frighteningly, the arrow of James's hidden dislike.

These vulnerable premonitions did not come to pass. Luckily, Miss Bosanquet had already left when Conrad knocked and James opened, and patted Conrad on the back, and led him in and stood him before the fire with many a "delighted to see you" and exclamations of "my dear good fellow" and worried inquiries about poor Mrs. Conrad's health, and exhortations to a libation of sherry, and urgings to take the chair that allowed a view of the grand edifice opposite, which housed the Turkish legation: a green crescent and a green star were painted on its roof. And then another knock, and it was Miss Hallowes, precisely as directed, bringing the latest portion of

the sea tale Conrad was thinking of calling "The Second Self,"
or "The Secret Stranger," though he might yet settle on something else . . .

"I'm much obliged to you, Miss Hallowes," he said, accept-
ing the moist folder; she had struggled to shelter it under her
coat. "Mr. James, may I present the very person your example
inspired? My amanuensis, Miss Hallowes, who flies off to enjoy her day in London, despite this wretched weather —"

Under her wet clumsy hat with its wet little feather, Miss
Hallowes's somewhat obvious nose reddened. She had a long
neck — she was long all over — at the base of which sat a bun.
The bun confined brown hair, the sort of brown that is so
common as to be always overlooked, except in a very pretty
woman. Miss Hallowes was not a very pretty woman. She was
thirty-seven, just starting a jowl. It was mostly inconspicu-
ous, but formed a soft round bulge whenever she lowered her
head. Her head, bending over the Machine, was usually lowered. Sometimes the quick agitation of her fingers and shoulders shook out her bun and uncaged it from its pins, and then
her hair would cascade down over her long back; she wondered if Mr. Conrad noticed. She had been employed by him
for the past six years, and was and was not a member of the
household — rather like a governess in a book. She often took
Borys to school. Yet after all this time Mr. Conrad still mis-
spelled her Christian name, and wrote it as "Lillian," with two
l's, when it had only one, and referred to her as his "girl." She
was gratified that he had not said "my girl" to Mr. James, who
was right now looking at her, or *into* her, with those lantern
eyes he had. He was much fatter than she had expected, and
showed a paunch and a developed jowl that reminded her hu-
miliatingly of the probable future of her own. She was dripping on his nice carpet; outdoors it was raining like mad; she
wished she could go stand in front of his fire. Her feet were

soaked through, and cold. But she was not to stay — she understood she was merely a necessary intrusion. If only Mr. James would not judge her by the ruin of her shoes!

She said, "How do you do, Mr. James," and moved to the door. Her hand was on the knob, but it was already vigorously turning, as if of itself, and a hand on the other side of the door slid through, and brushed against her own, and in leaped Miss Bosanquet.

"I do apologize, I was nearly on my way out — I seem to have forgotten my umbrella —"

The forgotten umbrella! Worn device, venerable ruse! Yet perhaps not — it was a fact, after all, that Miss Bosanquet, with James's permission, habitually kept an umbrella in his rooms. It hadn't been raining so heavily when she arrived at ten o'clock, and she was insouciant about such nonsense as getting a little wet — unlike some ladies, who behaved as if they were made of sugar and were bound to melt. But even Miss Bosanquet might acknowledge the need of an umbrella when the rain bounced upward from the pavement and a cutting wind pelted icy rivers into one's face: hence the contingency article in the Master's cupboard. The morning's drizzle had by now blown into a brutish January storm, which might very well explain why Miss Bosanquet burst in to fetch her umbrella just as Miss Hallowes was leaving, all inadvertently touching Miss Hallowes's large interesting hand.

Possibly there was another explanation. As Miss Bosanquet, having been discharged for the day, was passing through the monumental lower hall on her way out to the street, she heard a voice speaking the Master's name. A tall woman with a disheveled bun and wearing a charmingly silly hat stood at the concierge's desk, announced that she was expected, and asked where she might find Mr. James's apartment. She walked on through the hall's massive columns, halting to remove from under her coat a folder of the kind used to enclose manuscript. This was unquestionably odd: Miss Bosanquet was scrupulously cognizant of every sacred sheet of paper that entered or left the Master's sanctum; every hallowed word he breathed aloud danced through her agile fingertips and registered indelibly in her brain. Was this woman, apparently summoned by the Master, some hidden competitor? Under the excessive burden of preparing his strenuous New York Edition, did he feel that he required *two* amanuenses, one for the earlier part of the day, the other for the later? Miss Bosanquet was aware that she had had predecessors — and that she outshone them all: was there now to be a rival? For the too-costly MacAlpine the Master had found other employment, and Miss Weld had gone off in the bloom of her youth to be married. The last, a Miss Lois Baker, was sometimes called on, Miss Bosanquet knew, when she herself was compelled to be absent: could this be the same Miss Baker, harried and hurried, who was just then stopping to prop the suspicious folder against the base of a pillar while she rearranged the pins in her bun? She had loosened her hair; it swept free before she could scoop it up again, and in this one disclosing moment, when the length of it swung innocently by its own dark weight, Miss Bosanquet reflected that Miss Baker, if Miss Baker it was, resembled a mermaid all at once released from a spell — she was certainly wet enough! Were shining scales and a forked tail concealed, together with some errant manuscript, under her coat? Her long lurking body, like a mermaid cast up on solid earth, was spilling puddles on the marble floor. She had a broad shy mouth in a broad shy face, the sort of face you might see in an old painting of the Madonna, where the model had clearly been a plain peasant girl, coarse-skinned, yet with a transcendentally devoted mien. Miss Baker's eyes, if Miss Baker it was, were too small, and the lobes of her nostrils too fleshy, but standing there, with her hands lifted to the back of her neck, and looking all around, as if under the ceiling of some great cathedral, she seemed dutiful and unguarded and glowingly virginal. She picked up the folder and went on.

For ten minutes Miss Bosanquet lingered and pondered, lingered and pondered — and there *was* the question of the umbrella, was there not? So when she returned to the Master's rooms and dared to rush in, unexpectedly caressing the hand of the departing Miss Baker on the other side of the door . . . but no! It could not be Miss Baker, despite all. Miss Bosanquet was astonished to see that the Master, in the interim following her own departure, had received a guest, and the guest (impossible not to recognize him) was the renowned Mr. Joseph Conrad; and *therefore,* she instantly calculated, the manuscript the putative Miss Baker had been carrying pertained not to the Master, but to Mr. Conrad. Here was the proof: the folder was already in the grip of Mr. Conrad's nervously pinching fingers, and why was he pinching it in that strange way, and glaring at the two ladies as if they might do him some obscure harm?

It was done. It was inescapable. These women were not supposed to have met, and by the grace of God had eluded meeting — yet here they were, side by side: he almost thought he had seen them fugitively clasping hands. A baleful destiny works through confluences of the commonplace — that damnable umbrella! He pinched the folder Miss Hallowes had freshly delivered (she was punctual as usual), and pinched it again, pressing it hotly against his ribs — a shield to ward off that avidly staring Miss Bosanquet, who had the bright shrewd look of a keeper of secrets. What disadvantageous word, product of a supernal critical mind, had the Master confided in her? What fatal flaw — he was doomed to flaw, to sweat and despair — was she privately rehearsing, fixed as she was on this newest burden of his toil? That his tales were all Chinese boxes and nested matrioshkas, narrators within narrators, that he was all endlessly dangling strings, that he suffered from a straggle of ungoverned verbiage? In Miss Bosanquet's confident ease in the presence of the Master, he divined James's sequestered judgment — sequestered for the nonce, but might he not one day thrust it into print? *Mr. Conrad is to be greatly admired, but so flawed as not to be excessively revered.* Miss Bosanquet, who understood reverence, gave it all away in her long sharp look. And poor Miss Hallowes, with her little worshipful eyes (he sometimes suspected that he was worshiped by Miss Hallowes), what dour elements of his own sequestered view of the Master was *she* giving away? He wished they would vanish, the two of them!

But the Master came forward, and in his most expansively seigneurial manner introduced Miss Bosanquet to Miss Hallowes. "An unprecedented hour," he pronounced, "unforeseen in the higher mathematics, when parallel handmaidens collide. Can you hear, my dear Conrad, as thunder on Olympus, the clash of the Remingtons?" And when they were gone, Miss Bosanquet brandishing her retrieved umbrella, and Miss Hallowes in her dreadful shoes following as if led by an orchestral baton, he asked, "And do you find your Miss Hallowes satisfactory then?"

"Quite satisfactory," Conrad said.

"She discerns your meaning?"

"Entirely."

"Miss Bosanquet — you see how lively and rather boyish she is — yet she is worth all the other females I have had put together. Among the faults of my previous amanuenses — not by any means the *only* fault — was their apparent lack of comprehension of what I was driving at. And Miss Bosanquet is admirably discreet."

"One must expect no less."

"Miss Hallowes, I take it, you deem a *bijou.*"

"Indeed," said Conrad, though he remarked to himself that Jessie more and more believed otherwise.

⣷⣯

"Do give me your arm, or I shall never fit you under," Miss Bosanquet urged. "It's a wonder you haven't brought your own. Miss Hallowes, you're waterlogged!"

"I surely did set out with one, but the wind turned it inside out and swept it halfway into the square, and I couldn't go after it because Mr. Conrad so dislikes unpunctuality —"

"What a felicitous misfortune! The stars have favored us, Miss Hallowes — had you been delayed by a single minute, it's not likely that you and I should be splashing along arm in arm . . . I should so value half an hour with you — may I ask whether you have some immediate obligation —"

"I must look in on my mother, who hasn't been well."

"I plead only for half an hour. Shall we duck into the nearest Lyons and get out of the wet? I believe I am acquainted with every tearoom in the vicinity. I frequently bring Mr. James his morning crullers."

Miss Hallowes thought guiltily of her mother; but she was not so punctual with her mother as she was with Mr. Conrad. "It *would* be a pleasure to dry off my feet."

"Oh, your poor swimming feet!" cried Miss Bosanquet — which struck Miss Hallowes as perhaps too familiar from someone she had met not twenty minutes ago; and yet Miss Bosanquet's body was warm against her, holding her close under the narrow shelter of the umbrella.

When they were seated and had a pair of brown china teapots and a sticky sugar bowl between them, Miss Bosanquet asked, as if they were old intimates, "And how *is* your mother?"

"She suffers from an ailment of the heart. My mother is a widow, and very much alone. It is not only illness that troubles her. She is very often sad."

"Then how providential," Miss Bosanquet said, "to have a daughter to lighten her spirits —"

"They cannot be so easily lightened. My mother is in mourning."

"Her loss is so recent?"

"Not at all. It is more than five years since my brother died. For my mother the hurt remains fresh."

"Your mother must be a woman of uncommon feeling. And perhaps you are the same, Miss Hallowes?"

So suddenly private an exchange, and in so public a place! Though the few windows were gray and streaming, the tearoom's big well-lit space with its rows of little white tables was almost too bright to bear. She felt uncomfortably surrounded and pressured, and Miss Bosanquet was looking at her so penetratingly that it made her ashamed. Through some unworldly distillation of reciprocal sympathy, Miss Bosanquet was somehow divining her humiliation, and more: she was granting it license, she was inviting secrets.

"Your brother," she said, "could not have been in good health?"

"He was entirely well."

"I take it that he was cut down in some unfortunate accident —"

"He was a suicide."

"Oh my poor Miss Hallowes. But how —"

"He shot himself. In privacy, in the first-class compartment of a moving train."

All around them there was the chink of cutlery, and a shaking out of mackintoshes, and the collective noise of mixed chatter, pierced now and then by a high note of laughter, and the pungent smell of wet wool. Miss Hallowes marveled: to have told *that* about Warren, how unlike herself it was! But Miss Bosanquet was taking it in without condemnation, and with all the naturalness and practiced composure of a nurse, or a curate; or even some idolatrous healer.

"I understand perfectly," Miss Bosanquet said. "Your mother can hardly have recovered from such a tragedy. She leans on you? She depends on you?"

"All that is true."

"And she has become your life?"

"Mr. Conrad is my life."

Miss Bosanquet bent forward; the hollows in her thin cheeks darkened; her thin shoulders hovered over her teacup. "We are two of a kind, Miss Hallowes. You with Mr. Conrad, I with Mr. James. In the whole history of the world there have been very few as privileged as you and I. We must talk more of this. I presume you are living with your mother?"

"I have a flat in the Blessington Road, but I often stop with her for days at a time."

"And how did you come to Mr. Conrad?"

"I was employed by a secretarial office, and he found me there. He seemed pleased with my work and took me on."

"My own beginning in a similar office was, I fear, a trifle more devious. I deliberately trained myself for Mr. James. Certain chapters of *The Ambassadors* were being dictated from a stenographer's transcription. I heard that Mr. James was dissatisfied and in need of a steady amanuensis, and I set myself to learn to type. It was a plot — I schemed it all. You will judge me a dangerous woman!"

"You are very direct."

"Yes, I am very direct. I think you must begin to call me Theodora. For a very few friends I am Teddie, but you may start with Theodora. And what am I to call *you*, Miss Hallowes?"

Miss Hallowes gave out a small worried cough. She hoped it did not mean she was catching cold. She said, "I'm sure it's time I ought to be off to my mother —"

"Please don't evade me. We have too much in common. We are each in an extraordinary position. Mr. James and Mr. Conrad are men of genius, and posterity will honor us for being the conduits of genius."

"I never think of posterity. I think only of Mr. Conrad, and how to serve him. The truth is — I am certain he is aware of it — he said it outright in a letter to Mr. Pinker, a letter that I myself typed — he is so often unconscious of me, he never realized — he told Mr. Pinker that were he to allow it I should work for him for nothing. And I should. Besides, Miss Bosanquet —"

"Theodora."

"— Mr. Pinker is also a conduit, as you put it. All Mr. Conrad's work passes through him."

"And Mr. James's as well. But Mr. Pinker is merely a literary agent. Mr. Pinker is secondary. He is in fact tertiary. No one in future will know his name, I assure you. It isn't Mr. Pinker who is blessed to listen to the breathings, and the silences, and the sighs, and the pacings . . . sometimes, when Mr. James and I have been at work for hours, he will quietly place a piece of chocolate near my hand, and will even unwrap the silver foil for me —"

"There are occasions when Mr. Conrad is worn out at the end of the day and he and I sit in opposite chairs in his study and smoke. Mrs. Conrad doesn't like it at all."

"Smoke? Then you are an advanced woman!"

"Not so advanced as you, Miss Bosanquet — but you are very young and more accustomed than I to the new manners."

"*Theodora.* And I am past thirty. If by 'the new manners' you mean the use of our Christian names ... but look, our lives are so alike, we are almost sisters! It's unnatural for sisters to be so formal — have you no sisters?"

Miss Hallowes said gravely, "Only the two brothers, and one is dead."

"Then you will have a sister in me, and you may confide anything you wish. It's you who seem so young — have you never been in love?"

Miss Hallowes tried out her new little cough once more. It was not a cold coming on; it was recognition. Miss Bosanquet — *Theodora* — was entering a wilderness of strangling vines. In love? She believed, indeed she knew (and had declared it in Mrs. Conrad's hearing!), that Mr. Conrad's works were imprinted on her heart, and would remain so even after her death. The truth was she had loved him, mutely, for six whole years. Mr. Conrad never guessed it; he saw her, she supposed, as an enigmatically living limb of the Machine, and the operation of the Machine was itself enigmatic to him. But Mrs. Conrad, though simple and prosaic, had strong intuitions and watchful eyes, and ears still more vigilant. It had happened more than once that when Miss Hallowes and the family — it now included baby John — were at dinner, and if Miss Hallowes asked for the butter, Mrs. Conrad would turn away her head.

But she confessed none of this to, to ... Theodora.

She said instead, "You may call me Lilian, but please never Lily. And if you should ever write my name, you must write it with one *l,* not two."

"Then let me have your hand, Lilian."

Theodora reached over the sugar bowl and fondled the hand she had first touched on the other side of the Master's door. The palm was wide and soft and unprepared for womanly affection.

"Let us meet again very soon," she said.

෨෨

When Lilian parted from her mother that evening, it was later than she had expected. She had stopped at a butcher's for lamb chops, a treat Mrs. Hallowes relished, and cooked them, and tried to turn the conversation from Warren. Her mother's plaints inevitably led to Warren, and then, predictably, to Lilian and the usual quarrel. Warren had been thirty-seven when he shot himself ("when he was taken," her mother said), exactly the age Lilian was now. To her mother this number was ominous. It signified the end of possibility, the closing down of a life. The dark fate of the unmarried.

"Thirty-seven! It's no good to be alone, dear, just look at your own poor mum, without another soul in the house. I'd be stone solitary if you didn't come by. And there you are, shut up all day long with that old man, and what future are you to get from it?"

"Mr. Conrad isn't old. He's fifty-three, and has young children."

"Yes, and don't I always get an earful, Borys and John, Borys and John. You talk as if they're yours, getting them presents and such. That'd be well and good if you had one or two of your own. Every year you've spent with Mr. Conrad is a year thrown to the winds. I truly think he's wicked, keeping you confined, using you up like that —"

"Mother, please —"

"It's not that I haven't looked into that book of stories you gave me this last Christmas, when what I really needed was a nice warm woolen muffler —"

"Mother, I gave you the muffler too, and a pair of gloves, don't you remember? And you've got your new tea cosy right there on the pot."

"— that wicked wicked *Heart of Darkness,* such a horrifying tale I never in my life could imagine. What must be in that man's mind!"

"It's a very great mind. Mr. Conrad is a very great writer. Posterity will treasure him."

Posterity. How improbable: that formidable word, how it sprang out in all its peculiar awkwardness, not at all the kind of thing that fit her mother's kitchen — the very word Miss Bos . . . *Theodora* . . . had uttered only hours before.

"Well, there you're right," her mother said. "The man has sons, that's the only posterity, if you want to say it like that, any normal person ought to care about. And when you lose one of your own, like our Warren —"

Her mother broke into weeping, and Lilian felt relieved; she was not callous, but she was used to her mother's tears, and preferred them to the subject of a marriage that would never be.

ೲ

In her bed in the tiny flat in the Blessington Road, Lilian lay listening. She had hung a tall looking-glass on one wall to give the cell-like room an illusion of breadth, and from her pillow she could contemplate her reflection. She saw the white pillow behind her; she saw her head on the pillow. She saw her white face, dim in the half-dark, and (she fancied) ghostly. But she was not a ghost — she was ordinary flesh, as kneadable as dough, a woman's body alone in a bed, with her hand on her breast. A woman's hand, which no one had ever stroked — only that evanescent grazing at Mr. James's door, and that oddly enthralling caress across the tearoom table. Theodora had taken her hand and turned it over and over, and then comically pretended to read her palm, like a gypsy seer; and then she plaited her own hand through Lilian's, and looked at her ... how to say it? — cannily, almost tantalizingly, as no one had ever looked at her before; as if some unfathomable purpose were pulsing between them. Out of her pillow voices were rising, known and perilous voices: all week she had labored beside Mr. Conrad, capturing the slow windings of the voices as they came twisting out of his viscera, or else hurtled out in violent tornado coilings, so that her fingers had to fly after them, rattling the Machine, rattling the lamps, rattling Mrs. Conrad's porcelain figurines. They were the very voices she had carried that day to the Reform Club — the heart of a tale still uncompleted, not yet named. The voices were in her ears, in her throat, in the whorls of her fingers. *My double. My second self. My feeling of identity. Our secret partnership. My secret sharer.* The voices shook her, they frightened her, and when Mr. Conrad broke off at last, she saw how spent he was. She too was spent. He took out his flint lighter and put it back in his pocket. He wasn't getting it right, he told her, not even the title, and who knew when the thing might be ready for print? He would not smoke now — he was flushed and sickly and untidy, as though he had been vomiting all afternoon.

She lifted her hand from her breast, and with her other hand delicately, tentatively tapped it, patted it, smoothed it, ran her fingers along the knuckles and under the yielding arch of the palm — just so had Theodora played with her hand in the teashop, making a toy of it, and then, *then* — raising it, smiling and smiling, as if about to put the curious plaything to her lips. That knowing smile, and the surprising small shudder that crept along her spine — a woman seeming almost to wish to kiss a woman's hand! It stirred and troubled her — the sensation was so much like … that moment once, or moments, when, turning too hastily from the Machine to pass the day's sheaf of typed sheets to Mr. Conrad, a flurry of papers slipped from her, loosed and strewn, landing on the carpet, the two of them plucking and stooping and kneeling ("a pair of coolies in a rice paddy," he growled), their heads close and their hands entangled … The ends of his fingers were hard, and the veins in his wrists were thin blue ropes under her eyes: a sailor's worn claw, and the unforeseen movement of it, its gritty touch, rocked her and affected her with a kind of thirst. And there was Mrs. Conrad in the doorway, looking in angrily, and it was only Mr. Conrad holding out his hand to help Miss Hallowes up from her knees.

From the alley below her bedroom window — the filtering panes that sheathed her in a dusky mist of almost-light — Lilian heard a sharp clatter: a metal trash barrel overturned. The fox again, scavenging. A sly fox out of a fable, a fox that belonged in a wood — but there are sightings of foxes in the outlying streets of London, and once, coming home in the winter night from her mother's, she had glimpsed a brown streak under the lamppost; and then it was gone. And another time, in the early morning — the woman and the animal, both of them solitary, two stragglers separated from the pack, transfixed, staring, panicked into immobility. The fox's eyes were oddly lit, as if glittering pennies had got into its sockets; its ears stood straight up; its white tail hung low, like a shamed flag; its flanks trembled. A nervous wild thing. It twitched the upper muscle of its long snout — she saw the zigzag glint of teeth, the dangerous grin of ambush. How beautiful it was!

And the voices in the pillow persisted, growing louder with every repeated cry: *my double, my secret self, our secret partnership* ... In her dry-hearted bed Lilian held up her two hands and matched them one against the other, thumb to thumb, and observed how persuasively, how miraculously, they made an almost identical pair.

ℜ

What was most remarkable was that there was never a contest between them. They were not destined to be rivals or champions of rivals. In her very first note Theodora had insisted on this. The note was also an invitation: was Lilian fond of theater, and would she be willing to accompany Theodora to the Lyceum Tuesday next, to see Mrs. Patrick Campbell as Lady Macbeth? Lilian had promised to have dinner with her mother that evening, and how could she disappoint her? But she did, and her mother wept. Similar disappointments followed, until her mother's mood hardened still more, and her tears increased: it was nearly like losing another child, she said, since she was left to be abandoned and alone, with that unfeeling Mr. Conrad claiming Lilian's nights as well, and what a cruel waste of a young woman's life!

It was so jolly to be with Theodora — she truly was like a sister. In the theater, at the most shivery instant, when Lady Macbeth was gazing at her bloody hand and muttering "Out, damned spot," Theodora drew Lilian into her arms to shelter her from the fright of it, and this time really did kiss her, on her left temple, on her cheek, on her chin, and almost, almost on her lips. And Theodora had so many ideas for outings, some of them (or so it struck Lilian) just on the edge of risk or even threat. It became a teasing commonplace between them that Theodora was bold and Lilian was faint-hearted — though it was only Theodora who did the teasing, as if Lilian's reticence were merely a sham, since of course Lilian was the daring one: hadn't she agreed to come ice-skating, when she had never skated in all her life before? Teetering on the ice, Lilian's unaccustomed feet seemed to belong to someone else — the blades skittered uncontrollably, and her heart in its unfamiliar cavern vibrated madly — but Theodora's strong saving embrace was firm at her waist, and the warmth of her breath was feathery under her ear, laughing: "Oh my brave Lily, you're so red in the face you look positively painted!" It was the first time Theodora had called her Lily; she did not protest. After this, an excursion to the New Forest, where freshly falling snow obliterated the paths, and ownerless horses roamed free and untrammeled, sidling toward the human intruders and sniffing after crumbs with their dark vast smoldering nostrils and yolk-colored eye-whites and rolling imbecile eyeballs and gigantic mindless heads, as menacing as the massive mechanisms of train wheels seen too close.

There were parts of London Theodora knew, shadowy corners Lilian had never ventured into, and incense-stung cellars where motley strangers squabbled in raucous remote accents, like hotheaded revelers at an incomprehensible carnival. And sometimes the carnival turned up in Theodora's rooms at the top of an old row house, with a skylight, and on the black-papered walls murky blurry paintings that looked as if they had been dropped in a tub of water and got smeared all over. Women in rippling shawls, gripping the strawlike stems of wine glasses, moved stubbornly from painting to painting: each fiercely stained rectangle seemed an argument to be won. But at length these fearsome women went away, and Theodora said, "All this nice chardonnay left, and you haven't had a drop. I hope you haven't been brought up Temperance, Lil!"

"Mother and I used to take a beer or so with Warren, but never since. And Mr. Conrad, when he's not in company with ladies, prefers . . . well, the other sort."

"I won't ply you with whiskey, my dear, we'll leave that to the men, but wine you must have. One glass to gladden your heart, two to gladden mine."

Lilian obeyed and drank, with small hesitant sips. The moon was in the skylight, and the inky walls with their perplexing daubs pressed against her spine. She felt she had been lured to a far lighthouse built on a rock in the middle of a treacherous estuary. It was plain that Theodora had concocted all these unusual scenes and adventures to amuse and thrill her; she understood this — but why?

"Say Teddie and I'll tell you," Theodora commanded.

Lilian looked into her glass — the wine made a kind of mirror, a gathering of morning dews, and her eye lay dreaming there, pale as a lily and unexpectedly lovely, a tiny round calm pond lazily twirling, and unnaturally lit, like the fox's eye.

"Teddie," she said faintly, and let Theodora kiss her again, in her strange new way. She did not really like this — she did not like it at all — but she had a secret trick, a hidden lever at the back of her brain that she could raise or lower, nearly at will, whenever Theodora kissed her with that wary slow incautious kiss, as though unlatching a forbidden room. The trick was dangerous (everything that derived from Theodora was dangerous): Lilian touched the secret lever in her mind, and immediately Theodora became Mr. Conrad. Now and then a glowering unwelcome apparition wearing the face of Mrs. Conrad erupted on the underside of her tongue, and then Theodora was again Theodora; but most often Theodora's insistent mouth was wickedly transformed into Mr. Conrad's

—she could almost decipher his puzzling primordial Polish whisperings, and sense the wiry brush of his mustache.

The wine was drained; the moon too was drained from its surrounding glass. Under the blackened skylight Theodora was smiling her heralding smile. "You will remember," she said, "my admission the afternoon we met—"

"When you ambushed me," Lilian said.

"Yes, yes, you brazen thing, call it what you will. I've explained all that, and aren't you glad? We are friends, and sisters, and very soon we shall be sharers in a glorious act. It has only been a question of courage, of aspiring to courage, and there can be no aspiration without training. You recall," Theodora pressed on, "how I trained myself to become worthy of Mr. James. I wished to be the companion—yes, the companion!—of the greatest writer of the age."

Lilian said flatly, "Mr. Conrad is the greatest writer of the age."

"This will not be our quarrel. We shall have no quarrel at all. I believe I can boast that I have made you braver than you were—as one guides a lily afloat on a leaf into unknown waters. You have grown accustomed to the unaccustomed— even to a modicum of shock. You have been enrolled, you have been tutored, you have been apprenticed. I am happy that I have sometimes astonished you. But you must be braver now than you have ever been, if we are to have our success."

"To sit beside Mr. Conrad, and hear his voice each day of my life, is the only success I have ever desired."

"Lily, there is more. Much, much more."

"I want no more than I have."

"You do, Lily, you do. And you deserve more."

"I am merely an amanuensis. Why must I deserve more?"

"Because," Theodora said, "more is already in the power of your grasp. There is more to be had, if only we dare to take it.

Please note that I say 'we.' It cannot be achieved save in partnership. We are warp and weft, you and I. You are the lily, and I am the leaf that carries you."

Lilian took a breath; she was famished for air. Theodora was proposing ... what? That she become an accomplice of sorts, but toward what impenetrable end? Her pulse was quivering as it had quivered on the ice, but she hadn't really been frightened then, or in the theater (it was only Mrs. Patrick Campbell and some red stuff), or when the wells of the horses' nostrils blasted their steamy fumes, or among the Wiltshire steles in twilight, or in those cellars ... Everything Theodora had led her to was untried and unnerving and curiously beautiful, even when it was repellent (she thought of the fox and its creamy dark gums glimpsed above the spiky teeth); she had never been afraid of any of it. She was afraid now, when Theodora, taking her hand, went on turning it this way and that, turning it as she had done in the teashop long ago, as if she could turn away her fear.

"Think, Lily," Theodora urged, "you deem yourself 'merely' an amanuensis. Merely! I dislike this 'merely,' yet let us examine it. In all the past, has there ever been an amanuensis who has earned immortality? Who leaves a distinguishing mark on the unsuspecting future? One who stands as an indelible presence?"

Lilian withdrew her hand as if Theodora had set it on fire; she jumped up. "Is this a game?" she cried. "I am Mr. Conrad's secretary! Merely his secretary! It's Mr. Conrad who is immortal! His force, his vision! Why do you try to equate us, why do you trivialize?"

"Sit down, my silly Lily. You are too impatient—I am attempting to engage you in a profundity. I do not trivialize. We are speaking of the generations. If your Mr. Conrad should be venerated as far into the time to come as, let us say, the twenty-first century, then I concede he may be counted among the immortals. And Mr. James unquestionably. But are they interchangeable, these likely immortals? You must know Mr. James's belief — I hope I don't offend — so he once put it to me — that Mr. Conrad's novels on occasion take on the aspect of huge fluid puddings —"

"And for my part," Lilian retorted, "I have heard Mr. Conrad tell Mr. Wells that Mr. James's tales simply evade, that they leave behind no more than a phosphorescent trail —"

"Enough! And never mind. There will be no competition — I insist on it."

Lilian softened. Theodora was genuinely not looking to provoke. In her most teasing affectionate sisterly way, hadn't she called Lilian "my silly"? — the tenderest sort of chaffing. Besides, Mr. James and Mr. Conrad were indeed not interchangeable, Mr. Conrad being so much the superior. What Mr. Conrad knew of the sea, and of the ambivalence of men's souls! Whereas Mr. James was ... *American.* Theodora was threatening nothing — it was one of her larks, an innocuous game after all, a frolic, no different from that eccentric play of the kisses, or those confounding moments in the Stonehenge dusk once, when Theodora masked her face with her gloved hands and spread the fingers and peered through them as though each one were a small upright stone pillar, and ground out a mocking phantom Druid liturgy made up of coarse guttural lunatic syllables — so that Lilian, taken aback, had a little scare, until Theodora's laughter burbled out and left her feeling stupid. "It's your mother," Theodora chided, "your lugubrious mother — she's stunted you with all that gloom. She leaves you no space for mischief. Oh my poor Lily, when will you learn to play?"

So it was only play. A diversion. Fear? What was there to fear? But the skylight was as dense as the walls, oppressively so: the whole weight of stony astronomies seemed about to crash in on their heads. And here was Theodora, larking about with talk of eternal life for those forgettable wisps of ephemera who are faithful at their Machines day after day, typing, typing, typing, until they disintegrate into the dust of the earth . . .

"Think!" said Theodora. "Everlastingness for such as us! Who!"

Conciliating, Lilian overreached. "Boswell," she said finally.

"Boswell immortal? As an amanuensis? Never! An annoying sycophant. His only occupation was to follow in Dr. Johnson's wake, whether he was wanted or not."

"Still, he set down whatever Johnson spoke —"

"He wasn't wanted. Johnson didn't *choose* him. An amanuensis must be chosen. You and I, Lily, have been chosen. Try again."

Lilian released a dreary sigh. This diversion — this digression (but from what goal?) — was not to her taste. Perhaps it was true that like her mother — like Mr. Conrad himself! — she had been born to an uneasy lingering gloom. "Then Moses," she said, "who took dictation directly from the author. And was certainly chosen. Now there it is, done, your riddle is solved."

"Not satisfactorily. Truly," Theodora scoffed, "what have you and I to do with Moses? All those tedious Jewish rules! I ask you, my dearest Lily, why must we be confined by rules, when all the world's joy runs past them? I promised you a profundity. The chance lies before us — we shall be the first. If only you have courage enough, we two, separately and entwined, will live forever. Forever, Lily! The generations will *feel* what we do."

Under the skylight, opaque and invisible, and between the cryptic blotches on the walls, darkened now to a row of indistinct smudges (a single lamp stood in a distant corner), Theodora's look sent out a feral copper gleam. It came to Lilian then, sadly, horribly — oh, horribly — that it was not a game at all: she was being drawn instead into some dire scheme of an unbalanced spirit.

"No one," she said (and to her surprise, she heard her mother's bleak reproachful wisdom creeping up from her own throat), "no one can live forever."

But Theodora let out her jubilant larking laugh. "The Master will. Doubtless your Mr. Conrad will. And so shall we — we mere amanuenses. — Wait, Lily, where are you off to? We agreed you would stay the night —"

Lilian flung herself from Theodora's touch. "It's been weeks since I had a proper visit with Mother," she called back — what foolishness, it was two in the morning! — and hurried down the stairs.

෴

Theodora had frightened Lilian, but Theodora was, as it happened, altogether in her right mind. She was far from mad; she was consummately clever. Her stratagem was both ingenious and simple. And it was covert, designed to remain permanently undetected — this accounted for its originality. Also, it eschewed what has always been regarded as axiomatic: that immortality implies, and resides in, a name. Shakespeare is immortal, we say; and Archimedes, because his bath water spilled over, permitting him to dub the mess "physics." The Pyramids are rumored to owe their shape to Pythagoras and his hypotenuse. Shakespeare, Archimedes, Pythagoras, and any number of other luminaries (not forgetting James and Conrad) may all merit immortality in the ordinary sense — but Theodora's notion of everlastingness was more cunning than any such homage given to the longevity of a proper noun. What Theodora was after was distinctly radical: she wished to send into the future a nameless immutability, visible though invisible, smooth while bent, unchangeable yet altered, integrated even as it sought to be wholly alien. And it was to be secret. Nor could she accomplish it alone. It demanded a sharer, a double, a partner.

But meanwhile she had lost Lilian, and Lilian was indispensable for Theodora's plan. How to get her back? Four or five notes, wreathed in remorse and painted sunflowers (copied from one of those smeary foreign artists she incomprehensibly admired), went unanswered. It was a month before Lilian replied. Her tone was cool. Mr. Conrad, she explained, was keeping her exceedingly occupied; and her mother's spirits had sunk yet again, requiring Lilian's almost nightly attendance; and Mrs. Conrad had lately been particularly disagreeable. "I hope," the letter ended, "that in view of these increasing difficulties you will understand why I must discontinue our meetings, which by their nature distract me from my obligations and concerns."

Theodora was undiscouraged.

My dear Lilian [she wrote],
    Of the "difficulties" you allude to, surely your relation to Mrs. Conrad continues as the most onerous. I believe I can, even at this removal, discern what you must bear. A great man's wife, should he have one — and unlike Mr. James, Mr. Conrad is very much a married man! — will

too often be under the delusion that, by virtue of conjugal proximity, she can see into the heart of his genius. Yet how can this be? A shameful hubris! It is only you, the artist's true vessel, the sole brain to receive the force of creation in its first flooding, who can make this claim. A day may come — that day inevitably *will* come — when an imperious wife will publicly usurp your knowledge, your penetration, your having *inhabited* the work, and will profess to see and feel what you alone have seen and felt. What form this wrongful scizure will take, who can tell? In gossip to future biographers perhaps, in boastful letters (doubtless she already misleads Mr. Pinker), and, heaven forfend, even in a braggart's memoir from her own unskilled pen.

No, Lily, this cannot go forward. You must forestall such a devouring — it has the power to demean Mr. Conrad's art. You rightly speak of obligation and concern. *Here* must be your obligation and concern. Lily, come back to me! Together we will thwart these spousal depredations!

The response was quick:

Then you must make me a promise. You will no longer speak absurdly of the soul's afterlife — I hold with Mr. Conrad that we are tragic creatures destined to become dust. That is why his ambition is pure (it is the ambitiousness mortality confers), while Mrs. Conrad's is impure: it is, as you say, a lust to purloin, to burn with a stolen fire. — Secondly, though not secondarily, you will no longer press on me unfamiliar intimacies. If you keep to this agreement, I will consent to a resumption of our acquaintance.

How easily it was done! Theodora had won her back — wooed her, rather, through the bait of jealousy, that lowest of human passions. Lilian, Theodora concluded, was now sufficiently primed to collaborate — on the condition that Theodora would merely revise the footing of their connection. Easily, easily done! Lilian cannot be tempted by the sweet fruit of everlastingness? No matter: then she will be seduced by the bitter hope of undermining her persecutor. Lilian repudiates Theodora's kisses? Ah, but what transports are being granted elsewhere, and without the impediment of the other's reluctance!

In the weeks during which Lilian had absented herself, Henry James had received yet another eminent literary visitor: Mr. Leslie Stephen, accompanied by the younger of his two daughters. She had come to pay homage to the Master, who welcomed her charmingly, partly out of deference to her redoubtable father, a stern bearded figure with the bent back of a myopic scholar, but also because she had begun to acquire some respectable small notice of her own. At twenty-eight, she was already an accomplished critic. Theodora, watchful as she went on tidying the masses of papers surrounding her Machine, took care to observe Miss Stephen in particular. She was impatient and nervous, and appeared to be irritated by her father, who was enveloping their host in a burst of egotistical volubility. It was well known that Miss Stephen had a denigrating wit, and that she belonged to a notorious cenacle of youthful writers and artists, Fabians and freethinkers all, two or three of whom Theodora had encountered in those dusky contentious heterodox cellars. Miss Stephen herself was said to be melancholic and reclusive; even here, in this pleasant and spacious room, she kept her distance from her father, roaming disconsolately from the hearth to the window, where she took in with an indifferent blink the Turkish embassy's rooftop, and again back to the fire. Her troubled eyes were round and gray and judging, her throat was bare of any ornament, and she wore her hair in a softly sculpted chignon (a chignon as unlike Lilian's unreliable falling-apart bun as a croissant is different from a dumpling), so that in profile she had the look of a dreaming Aphrodite. An unprompted indulgence drew Theodora to the clear silhouette of that brow and nose and chin; but Miss Stephen's magnetism was reserved and unconfessed.

That same night (Theodora learned this only long afterward) Miss Stephen wrote in her diary: "Poor Mr. James eaten alive by Father today, who harangued incessantly, evidently taking the wrong side of the Conrad question. Miss Bosanquet rather handsome, an overvigilant coxswain in white shirtwaist and cinched blue skirt. For a loyal amanuensis she is not notably submissive. A sapphist, I wager."

Easily, easily done. Soon enough, Theodora had no further desire for Lilian's clandestine lips. She had Miss Stephen's. And when Miss Stephen became, of all things, engaged to a penniless Jew, she had them still.

꘎

Lilian was safe; she *felt* safe. She had abandoned Theodora and returned — it meant she had prevailed. She had warned Theodora, and Theodora had yielded. There were no more endearments, no more embraces, no more unwanted kisses. The kisses especially disturbed: they called up shivery hallucinations, illicit longings, and always at the rim of these, the threatening accusing glaring phantom of a scornful Jessie Conrad. It was a relief to be rid of them. And strange to say, Theodora in the relinquishment of these affectionate habits was as peacefully gratified as before, and even multiplied her smiles. With the kisses gone, so was that foolish talk of immortality, whatever Theodora had intended by it — it seemed to have nothing to do with heaven or angels.

Yet the plan was to go on precisely as it had first been conceived. It was only that they must now confront it through Lilian's eyes. "I have been too terribly selfish," Theodora said. "You were right to chastise me, Lilian. I have been forgetful of what you must be enduring —"

"It's not Mother I mind so much," Lilian said, mildly enough.

"Your mother's resentments are minor. Mrs. Conrad's are mammoth. She treats you as an appendage. A household tool, perhaps."

"She hates me," Lilian said.

"Then you will triumph in the end."

"In the end?"

"When our purpose is in place."

Cozening Lilian was becoming tedious. Theodora was restless: when *would* their purpose be in place? The beautiful task lay just ahead. She was eager to effect it, she had transformed its carapace to please her necessary confederate, and here was Lilian, dragging, dragging, perpetually in want of wheedling. It was difficult to be attentive: her innermost thoughts were dizzying, they were with Miss Stephen, who had begun to say Teddie, and Teddie had begun to say ... but meanwhile Lilian was reflecting that Theodora no longer cared to call her Lily, though once or twice the old companionable syllables slipped out, broken or misspoken, so that Lilian believed she almost heard — it could not have been — something that sounded like ... was it Ginny? Or was it Lily after all? Or *was* it Ginny? Or perhaps — but of course it must have been Geneva.

"That time in the hotel," Lilian joined in, "in Geneva, when Mr. Conrad had the gout again —"

Theodora stared. A lurking heat engorged her neck. The dream is father to the word: good Lord, had she actually pronounced Miss Stephen's name aloud? No, not her name exactly ...

"You remember, don't you, when he was wrestling with his anarchist story, three years ago or so, and Mrs. Conrad *would* insist on taking the children abroad, and the baby had the whooping cough, and Borys came down with a fever —"

"Geneva, yes," Theodora agreed, unbuttoning her collar — bloody hot or no, she must recover now — "you mention it so often. How Mrs. Conrad blundered."

"Interfered! Underfoot night and day with those sick boys, never permitting him to concentrate, despoiling his work —"

This, then, was the hour.

"And that is why," Theodora trumpeted, "it is imperative to defeat her. We are going to defeat her, Lilian," and at long last she defined her design.

☙

Theodora's plot.

Plot? Should art be dismissed as a conniving? The will to change nature's given is the font of all creation. Even God, faced with *tohu vavohu*, welter and waste, formlessness and void, thought it suitable to introduce light and dark, day and night: the seamlessness of disparity. Or regard the mosaic maker, painstakingly choosing one tessera to set beside another, in a glorious pattern of heretofore unimagined juxtapositions — yet because the stones as they were found have been disarranged, shall he be despised as a violator? If Theodora's scheme is sinful, let Michelangelo be ashamed: he prevails on God to touch Adam's finger. Like twinned with unlike is beauty's shock. And beauty, as Theodora knows, is eternal.

"Now first," she began, "you must tell me Mr. Conrad's procedure exactly as it occurs each day."

"He dictates, I type," Lilian said.

"Of course. And when do you present him with a finished typescript?"

"Never immediately. Sometimes our sessions are very long. Mr. Conrad rushes on, he puts up his hand as if to seize an elusive word out of the air. And sometimes — well, it can happen that he misspeaks an English idiom. Which, I will confess, I silently correct. Often I must retype a day's work several times in order to have a fair copy."

"All that is similar to my own experience with Mr. James. Mr. James, however, is beyond correction."

"Mr. James was not born in Poland."

"But he was born in America, which makes his intimacy with the English language all the more remarkable. Then you believe you have Mr. Conrad's trust?"

"Fully. Completely. I am confident of this. It's only Mrs. Conrad —"

"Very well," Theodora broke in. "This is what you will do, Lilian. I am to give you a passage — some sentences, let us say, or a paragraph or two — this remains to be decided upon. It will be selected from a singular work Mr. James is currently engaged in, a kind of ghost story, about a double, a man appalled by the encroachment of a second self —"

But Lilian gasped, "Why should you give such a thing to me?"

"You must listen attentively, or you will fail to follow. What I propose is not overly intricate, but it demands an orderly patience. We cannot allow missteps, we must be scrupulous. As I say, you will take from me a passage from Mr. James — an exquisite passage, I assure you — and in return I will receive from you some small striking extract from whatever work it is that occupies Mr. Conrad at present."

"Theodora, what nonsense is this, why are you making sport —"

"Mr. James's story is called 'The Jolly Corner.' What name does Mr. Conrad give his?"

"He has settled finally on 'The Secret Sharer,' and though it looks to grow long, it is not to be a novel. A tale rather, an astonishing tale, also about a double, how can this be! — but what has one to do with the other?"

"When we are done, everything. And if you are fastidious, it will yield everything you desire. Please hear me out. After we have made the exchange, you will carefully embed Mr. James's fragment in some hospitable part of Mr. Conrad's final copy, and I will insert Mr. Conrad's into a suitable cleft in Mr. James's manuscript. Now do you see?"

"Do I see? What *should* I see? A confusion, a scramble! What is to be gained by such mischief? Mr. Conrad reads over very thoroughly whatever I show him, and the fair copy when it is ready for print most thoroughly of all. Any foreign matter, whatever its intent, he will instantly detect, he will certainly excise it —"

"He will detect nothing. He will excise nothing. He will not perceive it as foreign matter. Nor will Mr. James."

"Mr. Conrad not to recognize what is and is not his own voice? How can you say this? What is to prevent him from discerning so bizarre an intrusion?"

"A lack of suspicion, a lack of any expectation of the extraneous. Simply that — and something still more persuasive. The egoism of the artist. The greater the art, the greater the egoism — and the greater the assumptions of egoism. Mr. Conrad will read — he will admire — he will wonder at what he believes he has wrought — he will congratulate himself! Privately, in the way of the artist in contemplation of his art. And there it will rest, what you call foreign matter, foreign no more, absorbed, ingested, seamless — a kidnapped diamond to shine through the ages, and you and I, Lilian, will have set it there!"

Theodora blazed; she was all theater; it seemed to Lilian that her fevered look, her shamelessly unbuttoned blouse, her untamed zeal, were more terrible than when Mrs. Patrick Campbell had pretended to be Lady Macbeth — but Theodora was not pretending.

In her mother's flat wail Lilian asked, "And will you also take Mr. James for a dupe?"

"Certainly not. Self-belief is no deception. It is how the artist's mind assimilates and transforms, and who has witnessed these raptures more than we?"

"But what you want from me is a deception all the same. Why do you suppose I care to have any part in it?"

"Because you do care. It means your triumph. Can't you *see*, Lilian? Mrs. Conrad exalts herself — how many times have I heard you complain of this?"

"I complain only of her presumption."

"Precisely. Her presumption in thinking that she has rightful possession of her husband's fecundity, that she is equal to its every motion, that she — she, a wife! — is the habitation of every word, and why? Because she sleeps in his bed. In his bed in the oblivion of night! — when it is you who in the light of day drink in the minutest vibrations of his spirit. What will Mrs. Conrad ever know of the kidnapped diamond? As long as you live, you will own this secret. If she demeans you, what will it matter? You have the hidden proof of her exclusion. Her exclusion! What deeper power than the power of covert knowledge? A victory, Lilian — see it, take it!"

Lilian was silent. Then "Ah," she murmured. And again, as if born for the first time into airy breath, "Ah."

Oh, easily, easily done! Lilian was satisfied, she was assuaged, she was enticed, she was caught; she was *in*. It was plain to Theodora that Miss Stephen ... *Ginny* ... could not have been won over so readily. Miss Stephen was not so pliant. Miss Stephen was prone to mockery — she was no one's confederate, she went her own way. Sometimes, she said, she could hear the birds sing in Greek.

ℰℛℴ

And so Theodora's determined map, with its side roads and turnings, proceeded.

"How fortuitous," she told Lilian, "to find ourselves so very far advanced even before we have rightly begun. We could not be better placed. This image of a strange and threatening alter ego — that two such illustrious minds should seize on an identical notion!"

"But Mr. Conrad's is a tale of the sea," Lilian demurred.

"That is why you must remember to keep clear of vistas — we cannot allow Mr. James's indoor characters to go wandering over Mr. Conrad's watery world. And the same with interiors: they must not fall into contradiction, a chimney-piece abutting a mast. As for names and dialogue, these too must be avoided —"

"If we are to omit all that," Lilian argued, "what remains to be extracted?"

The vexation of a dull counterpart. What would be the point of it all if the result were to fail of beauty, of artfulness?

"The heart, the lung, the blood and the brain!" Theodora shot out. "What we mean to search for are those ruthless invokings, those densest passages of psychological terror that can chill the bone. Pick out a charged exactitude, tease out of your man the root of his fertility —"

Theodora halted; she looked hard at Lilian: fearful dry celibate Lilian. How to arouse her to reckless nerve, to position her at the mouth of the beckoning labyrinth? To crank her imagination into life? She had been induced to favor the goal. She must now be induced to brave the dive.

"Lilian," Theodora dared, "I entreat you: squeeze out the very semen of the thing!"

Lilian neither blushed nor paled. "When we were first taken to see Warren's body, Mother and I," she said, "it was I who observed that the bullet, though applied to the head, had done exactly that. I have never forgotten the sight of it."

Theodora was chastened. "Then you are ready for our venture."

And still there were brambles and stiles on the way: the matter of timing, for one, impossible to predict or control. The synchronization vital to success. It was not a race, and even if it had been, it was scarcely likely that a pair of magisterial eminences would reach the finish line together. Now and again either Theodora or Lilian was obliged to temporize, and it happened once that Mr. Pinker received two notes only days apart, each puzzling over an untoward delay:

Dear Pinker,

Am being held up, though you should have the promised clutch of pages before too long. Miss Hallowes regretfully reports that her ribbon is fading toward illegibility. A fresh one awaits at the stationer's. In the meantime I am bursting with various damnations —

Yrs,
J. Conrad

My dear Pinker,

To attend most confidingly to your anxiety: Miss Bosanquet is indeed conscientiously aware of the exigencies of Scribner et al. I rely on her own admirable impatience — she assures me that she hastens, she drives on!

Yours faithfully,
Henry James

Nevertheless it is on an ordinary Thursday afternoon in the late winter of 1910 that the illumined moment strikes. It erupts with the miraculous yet altogether natural simultaneity of petals in a flowerbed unfolding all at once. Or else (so Theodora conceives it) as an ingeniously skilled artisan will slide a wedge of finely sanded wood into its neighboring groove to effect an undetectable coupling. Mortise and tenon! — the fit flawless, perfected, burnished. Or else (as Lilian, hesitant still, yet elated, sees it): like two birds trading nests, noiselessly, delicately, each one instantly at home.

In Henry James's London rooms a small dazzling fragment of "The Secret Sharer" flows, as if ordained, into the unsuspecting veins of "The Jolly Corner," and in Joseph Conrad's study in a cottage in Kent the hot fluids of "The Jolly Corner" run, uninhibited, into a sutured crevice in "The Secret Sharer." There is no visible seam, no hair's-breadth fissure; below the surface — submicroscopically, so to speak — the chemical amalgam causes no disturbance, molecule melds into molecule all serenely. And meanwhile Mrs. Conrad goes on sniffing and frowning in those leisured intervals when her husband and his amanuensis sit smoking together — but Lilian, far from cowering, only glows. And Theodora? — well, it makes up for fickle Miss Stephen's recent defection that Theodora has, after all, won more than an ephemeral kiss.

What has Theodora won? Exactly the thing she so resplendently envisioned: two amanuenses, two negligible footnotes overlooked by the most diligent scholarship, unsung by all the future, leaving behind an immutable mark — an everlasting sign that they lived, they felt, they acted! An immortality equal to the unceasing presence of those prodigious peaks and craters thrown off by some meaningless cataclysm of meteorites: but peaks and craters are careless nature's work, while Theodora and Lilian humanly, mindfully, with exacting intent, dictate the outcome of their desires. Lilian wills her hopeful fragile spite. Theodora commands her fingerprint, all unacknowledged, to be eternally engraven, as material and manifest as peak and crater. And so it is, and so it will be.

As for James and Conrad, in personal and literary character they are too unlike to sustain the early ardor of their long friendship. Though it has cooled, they are, if unwittingly, bonded forever: a fact in plain print, and in successive editions, that no biographer has yet been able to trace.

What is most extraordinary of all, however, is that Miss Bosanquet and Miss Hallowes, after the changelings were crucially implanted, never spoke another word to each other, nor did they ever meet again. It is probable that posterity, gullible as always, will suppose that they never met at all. But — truth to tell — posterity will have nothing in particular to remark of either one, there being no significant record extant.

NOTE: Among the historical actualities imagination dares to flout are club rules and death. Was Leslie Stephen in his grave nearly a decade before he makes his appearance here, and was no woman permitted to set foot in London's all-male Reform Club? Never mind, says Fiction; what fun, laughs Transgression; so what? mocks Dream.

ACTORS

Matt sorley, born Mose Sadacca, was an actor. He was a character actor and (when they let him) a comedian. He had broad, swarthy, pliant cheeks, a reddish widow's peak that was both curly and balding, and very bright teeth as big and orderly as piano keys. His stage name had a vaguely Irish sound, but his origins were Sephardic. One grandfather was from Constantinople, the other from Alexandria. His parents could still manage a few words of the old Spanish spoken by the Jews who had fled the Inquisition, but Matt himself, brought up in Bensonhurst, Brooklyn, was purely a New Yorker. The Brooklyn that swarmed in his speech was useful. It got him parts.

Sometimes he was recognized in the street a day or so following his appearance on a television lawyer series he was occasionally on call for. These were serious, mostly one-shot parts requiring mature looks. The pressure was high. Clowning was out, even in rehearsals. Matt usually played the judge (three minutes on camera) or else the father of the murder victim (seven minutes). The good central roles went to much younger men with rich black hair and smooth flat bellies. When they stood up to speak in court, they carefully buttoned up their jackets. Matt could no longer easily button his. He was close to sixty and secretly melancholy. He lived on the Upper West Side in a rent-controlled apartment with a chronic leak under the bathroom sink. He had a reputation for arguing with directors; one director was in the habit of addressing him, rather nastily, as Mr. Surly.

His apartment was littered with dictionaries, phrase books, compendiums of scientific terms, collections of slang, encyclopedias of botany, mythology, history. Frances was the one with the steady income. She worked for a weekly crossword puzzle magazine, and by every Friday had to have composed three new puzzles in ascending order of complexity. The job kept her confined and furious. She was unfit for deadlines and tension; she was myopic and suffered from eyestrain. Her neck was long, thin, and imperious, with a jumpy pulse at the side. Matt had met her, right out of Tulsa, almost twenty years ago on the tiny stage of one of those downstairs cellar theaters in the Village — the stage was only a clearing in a circle of chairs. It was a cabaret piece, with ballads and comic songs, and neither Matt nor Frances had much of a voice. This common deficiency passed for romance. They analyzed their mutual flaws endlessly over coffee in the grimy little café next door to the theater. Because of sparse audiences, the run petered out after only two weeks, and the morning after the last show Matt and Frances walked downtown to City Hall and were married.

Frances never sang onstage again. Matt sometimes did, to get laughs. As long as Frances could stick to those Village cellars she was calm enough, but in any theater north of Astor Place she faltered and felt a needlelike chill in her breasts and forgot her lines. And yet her brain was all storage. She knew words like "fenugreek," "kermis," "sponson," "gibberellin." She was angry at being imprisoned by such words. She lived, she said, behind bars; she was the captive of a grid. All day long she sat fitting letters into squares, scrambling the alphabet, inventing definitions made to resemble conundrums, shading in the unused squares. "Grid and bear it," she said bitterly, while Matt went out to take care of ordinary household things — buying milk, picking up his shirts from the laundry, taking his shoes to be resoled. Frances had given up acting for good. She didn't like being exposed like that, feeling nervous like that, shaking like that, the needles in her nipples, the numbness in her throat, the cramp in her bowel. Besides, she was embarrassed about being nearsighted and hated having to put in contact lenses to get through a performance. In the end she threw them in the trash. Offstage, away from audiences, she could wear her big round glasses in peace.

Frances resented being, most of the time, the only breadwinner. After four miscarriages she said she was glad they had no children, she couldn't imagine Matt as a father — he lacked gumption, he had no get-up-and-go. He thought it was demeaning to scout for work. He thought work ought to come to him because he was an artist. He defined himself as master of a Chaplinesque craft; he had been born into the line of an elite tradition. He scorned props and despised the way some actors relied on cigarettes to move them through a difficult scene, stopping in the middle of a speech to light up. It was false suspense, it was pedestrian. Matt was a purist. He was contemptuous of elaborately literal sets, rooms that looked like real rooms. He believed that a voice, the heel of a hand, a hesitation, the widening of a nostril, could furnish a stage. Frances wanted Matt to hustle for jobs, she wanted him to network, bug his agent, follow up on casting calls. Matt could do none of these things. He was an actor, he said, not a goddamn peddler.

It wasn't clear whether he was actually acting all the time (Frances liked to accuse him of this), yet even on those commonplace daytime errands, there was something exaggerated and perversely open about him: an unpredictability leaped out and announced itself. He kidded with all the store help. At the Korean-owned vegetable stand, the young Mexican who was unpacking peppers and grapefruits hollered across to him, "Hey, Mott, you in a movie now?" For all its good will, the question hurt. It was four years since his last film offer, a bit part with Marlon Brando, whom Matt admired madly, though without envy. The role bought Matt and Frances a pair of down coats for winter, and a refrigerator equipped with an ice-cube dispenser. But what Matt really hoped for was getting back onstage. He wanted to be in a play.

At the shoe-repair place his new soles were waiting for him. The proprietor, an elderly Neapolitan, had chalked *Attore* across the bottom of Matt's well-worn slip-ons. Then he began his usual harangue: Matt should go into opera. "I wouldn't be any good at it," Matt said, as he always did, and flashed his big even teeth. Against the whine of the rotary brush he launched into "La donna è mobile." The shoemaker shut off his machine and bent his knees and clapped his hands and leaked tears down the accordion creases that fanned out from the corners of his eyes. It struck Matt just then that his friend Salvatore had the fairy-tale crouch of Geppetto, the father of Pinocchio; the thought encouraged him to roll up the legs of his pants and jig, still loudly singing. Salvatore hiccupped and roared and sobbed with laughter.

Sometimes Matt came into the shop just for a shine. The shoemaker never let him pay. It was Matt's trick to tell Frances (his awful deception, which made him ashamed) that he was headed downtown for an audition, and wouldn't it be a good idea to stop first to have his shoes buffed? The point was to leave a decent impression for next time, even if they didn't hire you this time. "Oh, for heaven's sake, buy some shoe polish and do it yourself," Frances advised, but not harshly; she was pleased about the audition.

Of course there wasn't any audition — or if there was, Matt wasn't going to it. After Salvatore gave the last slap of his flannel cloth, Matt hung around, teasing and fooling, for half an hour or so, and then he walked over to the public library to catch up on the current magazines. He wasn't much of a reader, though in principle he revered literature and worshiped Shakespeare and Oscar Wilde. He looked through the *Atlantic* and *Harper's* and *The New Yorker,* all of which he liked; *Partisan Review, Commentary,* magazines like that, were over his head.

Sitting in the library, desultorily turning pages, he felt himself a failure and an idler as well as a deceiver. He stared at his wristwatch. If he left this minute, if he hurried, he might still be on time to read for Lionel: he knew this director, he knew he was old-fashioned and meanly slow — one reading was never enough. Matt guessed that Lionel was probably a bit of a dyslexic. He made you stand there and do your half of the dialogue again and again, sometimes three or four times, while he himself read the other half flatly, stumblingly. He did this whether he was seriously considering you or had already mentally dismissed you: his credo was fairness, a breather, another try. Or else he had a touch of sadism. Directors want to dominate you, shape you, turn you into whatever narrow idea they have in their skulls. To a director an actor is a puppet — Geppetto with Pinocchio. Matt loathed the ritual of the audition; it was humiliating. He was too much of a pro to be put through these things, his track record ought to speak for itself, and why didn't it? Especially with Lionel; they had both been in the business for years. Lionel, like everyone else, called it "the business." Matt never did.

He took off his watch and put it on the table. In another twenty minutes he could go home to Frances and fake it about the audition: it was the lead Lionel was after, the place was full of young guys, the whole thing was a misunderstanding. Lionel, believe it or not, had apologized for wasting Matt's time.

"Lionel apologized?" Frances said. Without her glasses on, she gave him one of her naked looks. It was a way she had of avoiding seeing him while drilling straight through him. It made him feel damaged.

"You never went," she said. "You never went near that audition."

"Yes I did. I did go. That shit Lionel. Blew my whole day."

"Don't kid me. You didn't go. And Lionel's not a shit, he's been good to you. He gave you the uncle part in *Navy Blues* only three years ago. I don't know why you insist on forgetting that."

"It was junk. Garbage. I'm sick of being the geezer in the last act."

"Be realistic. You're not twenty-five."

"What's realistic is if they give me access to my range."

And so on. This was how they quarreled, and Matt was pained by it: it wasn't as if Frances didn't understand how much he hated sucking up to directors, waiting for the verdict on his thickening fleshy arms, his round stomach, his falsely grinning face, his posture, his walk, even his voice. His voice he knew passed muster: it was like a yo-yo, he could command it to tighten or stretch, to torque or lift. And still he had to submit to scrutiny, to judgment, to prejudice, to whim. He hated having to be obsequious, even when it took the form of jolliness, of ersatz collegiality. He hated lying. His nose was growing from all the lies he told Frances.

On the other hand, what was acting if not lying? A good actor is a good impostor. A consummate actor is a consummate deceiver. Or put it otherwise: an actor is someone who falls into the deeps of self-forgetfulness. Or still otherwise: an actor is a puppeteer, with himself as puppet.

Matt frequently held forth in these trite ways — mostly to himself. When it came to philosophy, he didn't fool anybody, he wasn't an original.

"You got a call," Frances said.

"Who?" Matt said.

"You won't like who. You won't want to do it, it doesn't fit your range."

"For crying out loud," Matt said. "Who was it?"

"Somebody from Ted Silkowitz's. It's something Ted Silkowitz is doing. You won't like it," she said again.

"Silkowitz," Matt groaned. "The guy's still in diapers. He's sucking his thumb. What's he want with me?"

"That's it. He wants you and nobody else."

"Cut it out, Frances."

"See what I mean? I know you, I knew you'd react like that. You won't want to do it. You'll find some reason."

She pulled a tissue from inside the sleeve of her sweater and began to breathe warm fog on her lenses. Then she rubbed them with the tissue. Matt was interested in bad eyesight — how it made people stand, the pitch of their shoulders and necks. It was the kind of problem he liked to get absorbed in. The stillness and also the movement. If acting was lying, it was at the same time mercilessly and mechanically truthtelling. Watching Frances push the earpieces of her glasses back into the thicket of her hair, Matt thought how pleasing that was, how quickly and artfully she did it. He could copy this motion exactly; he drew it with his tongue on the back of his teeth. If he looked hard enough, he could duplicate anything at all. Even his nostrils, even his genitals, had that power. His mind was mostly a secret kept from him — he couldn't run it, it ran him, but he was intimate with its nagging pushy heat.

"It's got something to do with Lear. Something about King Lear," Frances said. "But never mind, it's not for you. You wouldn't want to play a geezer."

"Lear? What d'you mean, Lear?"

"Something like that, I don't know. You're supposed to show up tomorrow morning. If you're interested," she added; he understood how sly she could be. "Eleven o'clock."

"Well, well," Matt said, "good thing I got my shoes shined." Not that he believed in miracles, but with Silkowitz anything was possible: the new breed, all sorts of surprises up their baby sleeves.

Silkowitz's building was off Eighth Avenue, up past the theater district. The neighborhood was all bars, interspersed with dark little slots of Greek luncheonettes; there was a sex shop on the corner. Matt, in suit and tie, waited for the elevator to take him to Silkowitz's office, on the fifth floor. It turned out to be a cramped two-room suite: a front cubicle for the receptionist, a boy who couldn't have been more than nineteen, and a rear cubicle for the director. The door to Silkowitz's office was shut.

"Give him a minute. He's on the phone," the boy said. "We've run into a little problem with the writer."

"The writer?" Matt said stupidly.

"She died last night. After we called you about the Lear thing."

"I thought the writer died a long time ago."

"Well, it's not *that* Lear."

"Matt Sorley," Silkowitz yelled. "Come on in, let's have a look. You're the incarnation of my dream — I'm a big fan, I love your work. Hey, all you need is a Panama hat."

The hat crack was annoying; it meant that Silkowitz was familiar mainly with one of Matt's roles on that television show — it was his signature idiosyncrasy to wear a hat in court until the judge reprimanded him and made him take it off.

Matt said, "The writer's *dead?*"

"We've got ourselves a tragedy. Heart attack. Two A.M., passed away in intensive care. Not that she's any sort of spring chicken. Marlene Miller-Weinstock, you know her?"

"So there's no play," Matt said; he was out of a job.

"Let me put it this way. There's no playwright, which is an entirely different thing."

"Never heard of her," Matt said.

"Right. Neither did I, until I got hold of this script. As far as I know she's written half a dozen novels. The kind that get published and then disappear. Never wrote a play before. Face it, novelists can't do plays anyhow."

"Oh, I don't know," Matt said. "Gorky, Sartre, Steinbeck. Galsworthy. Wilde." It came to him that Silkowitz had probably never read any of these old fellows from around the world. Not that Matt had either, but he was married to someone who had read them all.

"Right," Silkowitz conceded. "But you won't find Miller-Weinstock on that list. The point is what I got from this woman is raw. Raw but full of bounce. A big look at things."

Silkowitz was cocky in a style that was new to Matt. Lionel, for all his arrogance, had an exaggerated courtly patience that ended by stretching out your misery; Lionel's shtick was to keep you in suspense. And Lionel had a comfortingly aging face, with a firm deep wadi slashed across his forehead, and a wen hidden in one eyebrow. Matt was used to Lionel — they were two old war horses, they knew what to expect from each other. But here was Silkowitz with his baby face — he didn't look a lot older than that boy out there — and his low-hung childishly small teeth under a bumpy tract of exposed fat gums: here was Silkowitz mysteriously dancing around a questionable script by someone freshly deceased. The new breed, they didn't wait out an apprenticeship, it was drama school at Yale and then the abrupt ascent into authority, reputation, buzz. The sureness of this man, sweatshirt and jeans, pendant dangling from the neck, a silver ring on his thumb, hair as sleek and flowing as a girl's — the whole thick torso glowing with power. Still a kid, Silkowitz was already on his way into Lionel's league: he could make things happen. Ten years from now the scruffy office would be just as scruffy, just as out of the way, though presumably more spacious; the boy out front would end up a Hollywood agent, or else head out for the stock exchange in a navy blazer with brass buttons. Lionel left you feeling heavy, superfluous, a bit of an impediment. This Silkowitz, an enthusiast, charged you up: Matt had the sensation of an electric wire going up his spine, probing and poking his vertebrae.

"Look, it's a shock," Silkowitz said. "I don't feel good about it, but the fact is I never met the woman. Today was supposed to be the day. Right this instant, actually. I figured first organize the geriatric ward, get the writer and the lead face to face. Well, no sweat, we've still got our lead."

"Lead," Matt said; but "geriatric," quip or not, left him sour.

"Right. The minute I set eyes on the script I knew you were the one. As a matter of fact," Silkowitz said, flashing a pair of clean pink palms, "I ran into Lionel the other night and he put me on to you."

These two statements struck Matt as contradictory, but he kept his mouth shut. He had his own scenario, Silkowitz scouting for an old actor and Lionel coming up with Matt: "Call Sorley. Touchy guy, takes offense at the drop of a hat, but one hundred percent reliable. Learns his lines and shows up." Showing up being nine-tenths of talent.

Matt was businesslike. "So you intend to do the play without the writer."

"We don't need the writer. It's enough we've got the blueprint. As far as I'm concerned, theater's a director's medium."

Oh, portentous: Silkowitz as infant lecturer. And full of himself. If he could do without the writer, maybe he could do without the actor?

Silkowitz handed Matt an envelope. "Photocopy of the script," he said. "Take it home. Read it. I'll call you, you'll come in again, we'll talk."

Matt hefted the envelope. Thick, not encouraging. In a way Silkowitz was right about novelists doing plays. They overwrite, they put in a character's entire psychology, from birth on: a straitjacket for an actor. The actor's job is to figure out the part, to feel it out. Feather on feather, tentative, groping. The first thing Matt did was take a black marking pen and cross out all the stage directions. That left just the dialogue, and the dialogue made him moan: monologues, soliloquies, speeches. Oratory!

"Never mind," Frances said. "Why should *you* care? It's work, you wanted to work."

"It's not that the idea's so bad. Takes off from the real thing."

"So what's the problem?"

"I can't do it, that's the problem."

Naturally he couldn't do it. And he resented Silkowitz's demand that he trek all the way down to that sex-shop corner again — wasn't the telephone good enough? Silkowitz threw out the news that he couldn't proceed, he couldn't think, except in person: he was big on face to face. As if all that counted was his own temperament. With a touch of spite Matt was pleased to be ten minutes late.

A young woman was in the outer cubicle.

"He's waiting for you," she said. "He's finishing up his lunch."

Matt asked where the boy was.

Silkowitz licked a plastic spoon and heaved an empty yogurt cup into a wastebasket across the room. "Quit. Got a job as assistant stage manager in some Off Off. So, what d'you say?"

"The part's not for me. I could've told you this straight off on the phone. The character's ten years older than I am. Maybe fifteen."

"You've got plenty of time to grow a beard. It'll come in white."

"I don't know anything about the background here, it's not my milieu."

"The chance of a lifetime," Silkowitz argued. "Who gets to play Lear, for God's sake?"

Matt said heavily, bitterly, "Yeah. The Lear of Ellis Island. Just off the boat."

"That's the ticket," Silkowitz said. "Think of it as a history play."

Matt sat there while Silkowitz, with lit-up eyes, lectured. A history riff for sure. Fourth, fifth generation, steerage troubles long ago strained out of his blood — it was all a romance to little Teddy Silkowitz. Second Avenue down at Twelfth, the old Yiddish theater, the old feverish plays. Weeping on the stage, weeping in all the rows. Miller-Weinstock ("May she rest in peace," Silkowitz put in) was the daughter of one of those pioneer performers of greenhorn drama; the old man, believe it or not, was still alive at ninety-six, a living fossil, an actual breathing known-to-be-extinct duck-billed dodo. That's where she got it from — from being his daughter. Those novels she turned out, maybe they were second rate, who knows? Silkowitz didn't know — he'd scarcely looked at the handful of reviews she'd sent — and it didn't matter. What mattered was the heat that shot straight out of her script, like the heat smell of rusted radiators knocking in worn-out five-story tenements along Southern Boulevard in the thirties Bronx, or the whiff of summer ozone at the trolley-stop snarl at West Farms. It wasn't those Depression times that fired Silkowitz — it wasn't that sort of recapturing he was after. Matt was amazed — Matt who worshiped nuance, tendril, shadow, intimation, instinct, Matt who might jig for a shoemaker but delivered hints and shadings to the proscenium, Matt who despised exaggeration, caricature, going over the top, Matt for whom the stage was holy ground . . . And what did little Teddy Silkowitz want?

"Reversal," Silkowitz said. "Time to change gears. The changing of the guard. Change, that's what! Where's the overtness, the overture, the passion, the emotion? For fifty, sixty years all we've had is mutters, muteness, tight lips, and, goddamn it, you can't hear their voices, all that Actors Studio blather, the old religion, so-called inwardness, a bunch of Quakers waiting for Inner Light — obsolete! Dying, dead, finished! Listen, Matt, I'm talking heat, muscle, human anguish. Where's the theatrical *noise?* The big speeches and declamations? All these anemic monosyllabic washed-out two-handers with their impotent little climaxes. Matt, let me tell you my idea, and I tell it with respect, because I'm in the presence of an old-timer, and I want you to know I know my place. But we're in a new era now, and someone's got to make that clear—" Silkowitz's kindling look moved all around, from desk to floor to ceiling; those hot eyes, it seemed to Matt, could scald the paint off the walls. "This is what I'm for. Take it seriously. My idea is to restore the old lost art of melodrama. People call it melodrama to put it down, but what it is is open feeling, you see what I mean? And the chance came out of the blue! From the daughter of the genuine article!"

Matt said roughly (his roughness surprised him), "You've got the wrong customer."

"Look before you leap, pal. Don't try to pin that nostalgia stuff on me. The youthful heart throbbing for grandpa's world. That's what you figure, right?"

"Not exactly," Matt fibbed.

"That's not it, honest to God. It's the largeness—big feelings, big cries. Outcries! The old Yiddish theater kept it up while it was dying out everywhere else. Killed by understatement. Killed by abbreviation, downplaying. Killed by sophistication, modernism, psychologizing, Stanislavsky, all those highbrow murderers of the Greek chorus, you see what I mean? The Yiddish Medea. The Yiddish Macbeth! Matt, it was *big!*"

"As far as I'm concerned," Matt said, "the key word here is old-timer."

"There aren't many of your type around," Silkowitz admitted. "Look, I'm saying I really want you to do this thing. The part's yours."

"A replay of the old country, that's my type? I was doing Eugene O'Neill before you were born."

"You've read the script, it's in regular English. American as apple pie. Lear on the Lower East Side! We can make that the Upper West Side. And those daughters — I've got some great women in mind. We can update everything, we can do what we want."

"Yeah, we don't have the writer to kick around." Matt looked down at his trouser cuffs. They were beginning to fray at the crease; he needed a new suit. "I'm not connected to any of that. My mother's father came from Turkey and spoke Ladino."

"A Spanish grandee, no kidding. I didn't realize. You look —"

"I know how I look," Matt broke in. "A retired pants presser." He wanted to play Ibsen, he wanted to play Shaw! Henry Higgins with Eliza. Something grand, aloof, cynical; he could do Brit talk beautifully.

Silkowitz pushed on. "Lionel says he's pretty sure you're free."

Free. The last time Matt was on a stage (televison didn't count) was in Lionel's own junk play, a London import, where Matt, as the beloved missing uncle, turned up just before the final curtain. That was more than three years ago; by now four.

"I'll give it some thought," Matt said.

"It's a deal. Start growing the beard. There's only one thing. A bit of homework you need to do."

"Don't worry," Matt said, "I know how the plot goes. Regan and Goneril and Cordelia. I read it in high school."

But it wasn't Shakespeare Silkowitz had in mind: it was Eli Miller the nonagenarian. Silkowitz had the old fellow's address at a "senior residence." Probably the daughter had mentioned its name, and Silkowitz had ordered his underling — the boy, or maybe the girl — to look it up. It was called the Home for the Elderly Children of Israel, and it was up near the Cloisters.

"Those places give me the creeps," Matt complained to Frances. "The smell of pee and the zombie stare."

"It doesn't have to be like that. They have activities and things. They have social directors. At that age maybe they go for blue material, you never know."

"Sure," Matt said. "The borscht belt up from the dead and unbuckled. You better come with me."

"What's the point of that? Silkowitz wants you to get the feel of the old days. In Tulsa we didn't *have* the old days."

"Suppose the guy doesn't speak English? I mean just in case. Then I'm helpless."

So Frances went along; Tulsa notwithstanding, she knew some attenuated strands of household Yiddish. She was a demon at languages anyhow; she liked to speckle her tougher crosswords with *cri de coeur, Mitleid, situación difícil.* She had once studied ancient Greek and Sanskrit.

A mild January had turned venomous. The air slammed their foreheads like a frozen truncheon. Bundled in their down coats, they waited for a bus. Icicles hung from its undercarriage, dripping black sludge. The long trip through afternoon dark took them to what seemed like a promontory; standing in the driveway of the Home for the Elderly Children of Israel, they felt like a pair of hawks surveying rivers and roads and inch-tall buildings. "*The Magic Mountain,*" Frances muttered as they left the reception desk and headed down the corridor to room 1-A: Eli Miller's digs.

No one was there.

"Let's trespass," Frances said. Matt followed her in. The place was overheated; in two minutes he had gone from chill to sweat. He was glad Frances had come. At times she was capable of an unexpected aggressiveness. He saw it now and then as she worked at her grids, her lists of synonyms, her trickster definitions. Her hidden life inside those little squares gave off an electric ferocity. She was prowling all around 1-A as if it was one of her boxes waiting to be solved. The room was cryptic enough: what was it like to be so circumscribed — a single dresser crowded with tubes and medications, a sagging armchair upholstered in balding plush, a bed for dry bones — knowing it to be your last stop before the grave? The bed looked more like a banquet table, very high, with fat carved legs; it was covered all over with a sort of wrinkly cloak, heavy maroon velvet tasseled at the corners — a royal drapery that might have been snatched from the boudoir of a noblewoman of the Tsar's court. A child's footstool stood at the bedside.

"He must be a little guy," Frances said. "When you get old you start to shrink."

"Old-timer," Matt spat out. "Can you imagine? That's what he called me actually."

"Who did?"

"That twerp Silkowitz."

Frances ignored this. "Get a look at that bedspread or whatever it is. I'd swear a piece of theater curtain. And the bed! Stage furniture. Good God, has he read all this stuff?"

Every space not occupied by the dresser, the chair, and the bed was tumbled with books. There were no shelves. The books rose up from the floorboards in wobbly stacks, with narrow aisles between. Some had fallen and lay open like wings, their pages pulled from their spines.

"German, Russian, Hebrew, Yiddish. A complete set of Dickens. Look," Frances said, *"Moby-Dick!"*

"In the atrium they told me visitors," said a voice in the doorway. It was the brassy monotone of the almost-deaf, a horn bereft of music. Frances hiked up her glasses and wiped her right hand on her coat: *Moby-Dick* was veiled in grime.

"Mr. Miller?" Matt said.

"Bereaved, sir. Eli Miller is bereaved."

"I heard about your daughter. I'm so sorry," Matt said; but if this was going to be a conversation, he hardly knew how to get hold of it.

The old man was short, with thick shoulders and the head of a monk. Or else it was Ben Gurion's head: a circle of naked scalp, shiny as glass, and all around it a billowing ring of pearl-white hair, charged with static electricity. His cheeks were a waterfall of rubbery creases. One little eye peeped out from the flow, dangerously blue. The other was sealed into its socket. You might call him ancient, but you couldn't call him frail. He looked like a man who even now could take an ax to a bull.

He went straight to the stepstool, picked it up, and tossed it into the corridor; it made a brutal clatter.

"When I go out they put in trash. I tell them, Eli Miller requires no ladders!" With the yell of the deaf he turned to Frances. "She was a woman your age. What, you're fifty? Your father, he's living?"

"He died years ago," Frances said. Her age was private; a sore point.

"Naturally. This is natural, the father should not survive the child. A very unhappy individual, my daughter. Divorced. The husband flies away to Alaska and she's got her rotten heart. A shame, against nature — Eli Miller, the heart and lungs of an elephant! Better a world filled with widows than divorced." He curled his thick butcher's arm around Frances's coat collar. "Madam, my wife if you could see her you would be dumbstruck. She had unusually large eyes and with a little darkening of the eyelids they became larger. Big and black like olives. Thirty-two years she's gone. She had a voice they could hear it from the second balcony, rear row."

Matt caught Frances's look: it was plain she was writing the old fellow off. *Not plugged in,* Frances was signaling, *nobody home upstairs, lost his marbles.* Matt decided to trust the better possibility: a bereaved father has a right to some indulgence.

"There's real interest in your daughter's play," he began; he spoke evenly, reasonably.

"An ambitious woman. Talent not so strong. Whoever has Eli Miller for a father will be ambitious. Eli Miller's talent, this is another dimension. What you see here"— he waved all around 1-A —"are remnants. Fragments and vestiges! *The Bewildered Bridegroom,* 1924!" He pinched a bit of the maroon velvet bedspread and fingered its golden tassel. "From the hem of Esther Borodovsky's dress hung twenty-five like this! And four hundred books on the walls of Dr. Borodovsky! That's how we used to do it, no stinginess! And who do you think played the Bridegroom? Eli Miller! The McKinley Square Theater, Boston Road and 169th, they don't forget such nights, whoever was there they remember!"

Matt asked, "You know your daughter wrote a play? She told you?"

"And not only the Bridegroom! Othello, Macbeth, Polonius. Polonius the great philosopher, very serious, very wise. Jacob Adler's Shylock, an emperor! Tomashefsky, Schwartz, Carnovsky!"

"Matt," Frances whispered, "I want to leave *now.*"

Matt said slowly, "Your daughter's play is getting produced. I'm *in* it. I'm an actor."

The old man ejected a laugh. His dentures struck like a pair of cymbals; the corona of his magnetic hair danced. "Actor, actor, call yourself what you want, only watch what you say in front of Eli Miller! My daughter, first it's *romanen,* now it's a play! Not only is the daughter taken before the father but also the daughter is mediocre. Always mediocre. She cannot ascend to the father! Eli Miller the pinnacle! The daughter climbs and falls. Mediocre!"

"Matt, let's go," Frances growled.

"And this one?" Again the old man embraced her; Frances recoiled. "This one is also in it?"

"Here," Matt said, and handed Eli Miller one of Teddy Silkowitz's cards. "If you want to know more, here's the director." He stopped; he thought better of what he was about to say. But he said it anyway: "He admires your daughter's work."

"Eli Miller's Polonius, in the highest literary Yiddish, sir! Standing ovations and bravo every night. Every matinee. Three matinees a week, that's how it was. Bravo bravo. By the time she's born, it's after the war, it's 1948, it's finishing up, it's practically gone. Gone — the whole thing! After Hitler, who has a heart for tragedy on a stage? Anyhow no more actors, only movie stars. Please, sir, do me a favor and name me no names, what is it, who is it, who remembers? But Eli Miller and Esther Borodovsky, also Dr. Borodovsky, whoever was there they remember!"

"With or without you," Frances warned, "I'm going."

Matt hung on. "Your daughter's play," he said, "is out of respect for all that. For everything you feel."

"What are you saying? I know what she is! My daughter, all her life she figures one thing, to take away Eli Miller's soul. This is why God makes her mediocre, this is why God buries the daughter before the father!"

They left him with tears running out of the one blue eye.

"I think you incited him," Frances said. "You just went ahead and provoked him." They were huddled in the bus shelter, out of the wind. It was five o'clock and already night.

Matt said, "An old actor, maybe he was acting."

"Are you kidding?" Frances said; hunched inside the bulk of her coat, she was shivering.

"You're always telling me *I* do that."

"Do what?"

"Act all the time."

"Oh, for Pete's sake," Frances said. "Why did you make me come anyhow? My toes are numb."

Late in February, a day of falling snow, rehearsals began. Silkowitz had rented a cellar in a renovated old building in the West Forties, in sight of the highway and the river. The space had a stage at one end and at the other a sort of stockade surrounding a toilet that occasionally backed up. The ceiling groaned and shuddered. A far-off piano thumped out distracting rhythms: there was a dance studio overhead. The cast was smaller than Matt had expected — the three female roles had been reduced to two. Silkowitz had spent the past month reviewing the script, and was still not satisfied. No sooner did Matt learn the moves of a scene than the director had second thoughts and rearranged the blocking. To Matt's surprise, the boy who had been in Silkowitz's office was there, presiding over a notebook; Silkowitz had brought him back to be stage manager. Matt calculated that the kid had six weeks' experience.

Silkowitz had put himself in charge of secrets. Each rehearsal session felt like a cabal from which the actors were excluded. Strangers came and went, carrying portfolios. Silkowitz never introduced any of them. "This is going to be a tight job, nothing extraneous. I believe in collaboration with all my heart, but just remember that collaboration runs through me," he announced. And another time: "My intention is to clot the curds." It was a tyranny that outstripped even Lionel's. The veneer was on the shabby side, but there was a stubborn complacency beneath. Matt, who had his own ideas and liked to cavil, was disinclined to argue with Silkowitz. The director would stop him mid-sentence to murmur against a wall with one of those coming and going unknowns: it was a discussion of the set, or some question about the lighting; or there would be the incidental music to consider. The house was already booked, Silkowitz reported — a two-hundred-and-ninety-nine-seater west of Union Square — and he had nailed down a pair of invisible backers, whom he did not name. Silkowitz had a reputation for working fast: what seemed important yesterday no longer mattered today. He scarcely listened when Matt began to tell about the visit to Eli Miller. "Good, good," he replied, "right," and turned away to look over someone's swatch of cloth. It was as if he had never insisted on the journey to the Home for the Elderly Children of Israel.

At the end of each day's rehearsal, the director sat on the edge of the stage and drew the actors around him in a half-circle and gave them his notes. And then came the daily exhortation: what he wanted from them all, he said, was more passion, more susceptibility. He wanted them to be drinking metaphorical poison; he wanted them to pour out blood and bile and bitter gall.

"Especially you, Matt. You're underplaying again. Forget that less-is-more business, it's crap! More energy! We've got to hear the thunderclap."

Matt's throat hurt. He was teaching himelf to howl. He had abandoned all his customary techniques: his vocal cords seemed perplexed by these new uses. He felt his chest fill with a curious darkness. In the morning, before taking the subway down to rehearsal, he tramped through the blackening snow to the public library and found a warm spot near a radiator and fell into *King Lear,* the original. He saw how those selfish women were stripping the old guy to the bone — no wonder he howls!

He was heading back to the subway when it occurred to him that it was weeks since he had stepped into the shoe-repair shop.

Salvatore did not know him.

"Hey, Salvatore!" Matt called in that stagy roar Silkowitz liked, and attempted an abbreviated version of his little comic jig. But in his clumsy buckled-up snow boots he could only stamp.

Salvatore said over the noise of his machines, "You got shoes to fix, mister?"

"What's the matter with *you?*" Matt said.

"*Il attore!*"

The trouble was the beard, the shoemaker said. Who could see it was his friend Matteo? What was the beard *for?* Had he gone into opera after all? With the beard he looked one hundred years old. This frightened Matt. Just as Silkowitz had predicted, Matt's whiskers had grown in stark white: he was passing for an old-timer in earnest.

And it was true: in a way he *had* gone into opera. Marlene Miller-Weinstock's primal voice still reverberated, even with Silkowitz's changes. His changes were logistical: he had moved the locale, updated the era, and accommodated the names of the characters to contemporary ears. Marlene Miller-Weinstock's play was a kind of thirties costume drama, and Silkowitz had modernized it. That was all. The speeches were largely unaltered. Grandiloquence! There were no insinuations or intimations, none of those shrewd hesitations Matt loved to linger over. His gods were ellipsis and inference. Hers were bombast and excitation. Matt's particular skill was in filling in the silent spaces: he did it with his whole elastic face, and in the stance of his legs — a skeptical tilt of knee, an ironical angle of heel. But Marlene Miller-Weinstock's arias left no room for any play of suggestion or uncertainty. Fury ruled; fury and conviction and a relentless and fiery truth. It came to Matt that fury *was* truth; it amazed him that this could be so. His actor's credo had always been the opposite: glimmer and inkling are truth, hint and intuition are truth; nuance is essence. What Marlene Miller-Weinstock was after was malevolence, rage, even madness: vehemence straight out; shrieks blasted from the whirlwind's bowel. She was all storm. In the gale's wild din — inside all that howling — Matt was learning how to hear the steady blows of some interior cannon. The booms were loud and regular: it was his own heartbeat.

Those two women with him on that dusty ill-lit stage — he felt apart from them, he saw them as moving shadows of himself. He felt apart from the men, one of whom he had worked with before, under Lionel's direction. And in the darkened margins of the place, on folding chairs along the wall, here was the boy with his notebook, and Silkowitz next to him, faintly panting, kicking his foot up and down as if marching to an unheard band. But Matt had pushed through a vestibule of embarrassment (it was shame over being made to howl) into some solitary chamber, carpeted and tapestried; it was as if he had broken through a membrane, a lung, behind which a sudden altar crouched, covered with Eli Miller's heavy tasseled bedspread. In this chamber Matt listened to his heartbeat. He understood that it wasn't Silkowitz who had led him here. Silkowitz was a literalist, a sentimentalist, a theorist — one of these, or all. Mainly he was flashy. Silkowitz's bets were on the future. He had nothing to do with this voluptuous clamor, Matt inside the gonging of his own rib cage, alone and very large; terrifyingly huge there on that dusty ill-lit stage. Marlene Miller-Weinstock had drawn him in. Or her father had. Inside his howl, Matt was beginning to believe the father's accusation: the daughter had taken hold of the father in order to copy his soul.

Silkowitz was pleased. "You've got it together," he told Matt. "Stick with Matt," he said to the others. He praised Matt for being everywhere at once, like a rushing ghost; for looking into the women's eyes with a powerful intimacy beyond naturalism; for what he called "symbolic stature" and "integration into the scene." All this puzzled Matt. He hated the lingo. It wasn't what he was feeling, it wasn't what he was doing. He had no consciousness of being part of a company. He wasn't serving the company, whatever Silkowitz might think. He was in pursuit of his grand howl. He wanted to go on living inside it. When rehearsals were over he kept to himself and hurried to the subway.

Ten days before the opening, Silkowitz moved the cast to the theater. It was a converted movie house; the stage was undersized but workable. To get to the men's dressing room you had to go through a narrow airless tunnel with great rusted pipes sweating overhead. The place was active, swarming. The boy with the notebook kept on checking his lists and schedules; he seemed professional enough. Wires crisscrossed the floor. Taped music traveled on phantom waves between scenes. Big wooden shapes materialized, pushed back and forth along the apron. Silkowitz had a hand in everything, running from corner to corner, his long girlish hair rippling, the silver thumb ring reddening in the light of the Exit sign whenever he glided past it.

Frances had decided to attend these final days of rehearsal. Silkowitz made no objection. She came hauling a tote bag, and settled into the next-to-last row, laying out her diction-aries and references and pencils on the seats around her. She worked quietly, but Matt knew she was attentive and worried. He was indifferent to her inspections and judgments; he was concentrating on his howl. She mocked it as rant, but it didn't trouble her that Matt had departed from his usual style — he was doing his job, he was giving the director what he wanted. What it meant was a paycheck. And by now Matt couldn't claim, either, that Silkowitz was egging him on. The director was taking in whatever Matt was emitting. He was emitting a sea of lamentation. Frances dumped her papers back into the tote and listened. Matt was standing downstage, alone, in pro-file, leaning forward like a sail in the wind, or like the last leaf of a wintry tree. He looked wintry himself. It was the day's concluding run-through; the rest of the cast had left. Matt was doing his solo scene near the end of the second act. His big belly had mostly sunk. Lately he had no appetite. He was never hungry. His beard had lengthened raggedly; a brown-ish-yellowish tinge showed at the tips. He seemed mesmer-ized, suffering. He was staring ahead, into the dark of the wings.

He turned to Silkowitz. "Someone's out there," he said.

"There shouldn't be," Silkowitz said. "Sally's kid's sick, she went home. And anyhow her cue brings her in the other way. Is that electrician still working back there?" he called to the boy with the notebook.

"Everyone's gone," the boy called back.

Matt said hoarsely, "I thought I saw someone." He had let his hair grow down to meet the beard. His eyes were birdlike, ringed with creases.

"O.K., call it a day. You're not the only one who's dead tired," Silkowitz said. "Go get some sleep."

On the way to the subway, Frances beside him, Matt

brooded. "There was a guy out there. He was coming from the men's toilet, I saw him."

"It's the neighborhood. Some creep wandered in."

"He was there yesterday too. In the middle of that same speech. I think someone's hiding out."

"Where? In the men's toilet?"

"Ever since we got to the theater. I saw him the first day."

"You never said anything."

"I wasn't sure he was there."

He was sorry he had spoken at all. It wasn't something he wanted to discuss with Frances. She had ridiculed his howl; now she was telling him it was worse than rant, he was hamming it up. The ignorance, the obtuseness! He was seized, dissolved, metamorphosed. His howl had altered him: the throat widens and becomes a highway for specters, the lungs an echo chamber for apparitions. His howl had floated him far above Frances, far above Silkowitz. Silkowitz and Lionel, what did it matter? They were the same, interchangeable, tummlers and barkers, different styles, what did it matter? Silkowitz was attracted to boldness and color, voices as noisy as an old music hall; he was as helpless as Frances to uncover what lay in the cave of the howl. As for the actors, Matt saw them as automatons; he was alone, alone. Except for the man who was hiding out, lurking, gazing.

"My God, Matt," Frances exploded, "you're hallucinating all over the place. It's enough you've started to *look* the part, you don't have to go crazy on top of it. Don't expect me to go there again, I'm keeping away, I've got my deadlines anyhow."

That night her grids sprouted "urus," "muleta," "athanor," "stammel," "nystagmic," "mugient." She worked into the dawn and kept her head down. Occasionally she stopped to polish her lenses. Matt knew her to be inexorably logical.

. . .

The day before dress rehearsal, Matt brought his shoes in for a shine. Salvatore seemed wary. Matteo, he said, no longer looked one hundred years old; he looked two hundred.

"You know," Matt said carefully— he had to whisper now to preserve his howl—"there's something better than opera."

Salvatore said there was nothing better than opera. What could be better than opera? For the first time he let Matt pay for his shine.

Dress rehearsal went well, though a little too speedily. The man in the wings had not returned. Silkowitz sat with the cast and gave his last notes. He did not address Matt. Odors of coffee and pastries wafted, and with unexpected lust Matt devoured a bagel spread with cream cheese. He understood himself to be in possession of a deep tranquility. All around him there was nervous buffoonery, witticisms, unaccount- able silliness; it was fruition, it was anticipation. The director joined in, told jokes, teased, traded anecdotes and rumors. A journalist, a red-haired woman from the *Times,* arrived to in- terview Silkowitz. He had hired an industrious publicist; there had been many such journalists. This one had just come from speaking to Lionel, she said, to cover the story from another angle: how, for instance, a more traditional director might view the goings-on down near Union Square. Lionel had re- sponded coolly: he was a minimalist; he repudiated what he took to be Teddy Silkowitz's gaudy postmodern experimen- talism. Would he show up at the opening? No, he thought not.

"He'll be here," Silkowitz told the interviewer. The lit- tle party was breaking up. "And don't I know what's bugging him. He used to do this sort of thing himself. He was a child actor at the old Grand Theater downtown."

"Oh, come on. Lionel's an Anglophile."

"I read up on it," Silkowitz assured her. "In 1933 he played the boy Shloymele in *Mirele Efros*. God forbid anybody should find out."

The cast, packing up to go home, laughed; wasn't this one of Silkowitz's show-biz gags? But Matt was still contemplating the man in the wings. He had worked himself up to unhealthy visions. It was likely that Frances was right; at least she was sensible. Someone had sneaked in from the street. A homeless fellow sniffing out a warm corner to spend the night. A drunk in need of a toilet. Or else a stagehand pilfering cigarettes on the sly. A banner, a rope, an anything, swaying in the narrow wind that blew through a crack in the rafters. Backstage — deserted at the end of the day, inhabited by the crawling dark.

On the other hand, he knew who it was; he knew. It was the old guy. It was Eli Miller, come down on the M-4 bus from his velvet-curtained bed in the Home for the Elderly Children of Israel.

Lionel would keep his word. He would stay away. Matt had his own thoughts about this, on a different track from Silkowitz's. Matt as Lear! Or a kind of Lear. Lionel had never given Matt the lead in anything; he was eating crow. Naturally he wouldn't put in an appearance. Thanks to Marlene Miller-Weinstock — swallowing her father's life, vomiting out a semblance of Lear — it was a case of Matt's having the last laugh.

In the clouded dressing-room mirror, preparing during intermission for the second act, he thickened his eyebrows with paint and white gum and spilled too much powder all over his beard — the excesses and accidents of opening night. He stepped out of his newly polished shoes to stand on bare feet and then pulled on his costume: a tattered monkish robe. Sackcloth. A tremor shook his lip. He examined the figure in the mirror. It was himself, his own horrifying head. He resembled what he remembered of Job—diseased, cut down, humiliated. The shoemaker if he could see him would add another hundred years.

The first act had survived the risks. Silkowitz had all along worried that the audience, rocked by the unfamiliar theatricality —the loudness, the broadness, the brazenness, the bigness— would presume something farcical. He was in fear of the first lone laugh. A shock in the serpent's tail pulses through to its tongue. An audience is a single beast, a great vibrating integer, a shifting amoeba without a nucleus. One snicker anywhere in its body can set off convulsions everywhere, from the orchestra to the balcony. Such were the director's sermons, recounting the perils ahead; Matt habitually shut out these platitudes. And more from that cornucopia—think of yourselves, Silkowitz lectured them all, as ancient Greek players on stilts, heavily, boldly masked; the old plays of Athens and the old plays of Second Avenue are blood cousins, kin to kin. Power and passion! Passion and power!

Were they pulling it off? During the whole first act, a breathing silence.

Sweating, panting his minor pant, Silkowitz came into the dressing room. Matt turned his back. A transgression. An invasion. Where now was that sacred stricture about the inviolability of an actor's concentration in the middle of a performance, didn't that fool Silkowitz know better? A rip in the brain. Matt was getting ready to lock it up—his brain; he was goading it into isolation, into that secret chamber, all tapestried and tasseled. He was getting ready to enter his howl, and here was Silkowitz, sweating, panting, superfluous, what was he doing here, the fool?

"Your wife said to give you this." Silkowitz handed Matt a folded paper. He recognized it as a sheet from the little spiral pad Frances always carried in her pocketbook. It was her word-collector.

"Not now. I don't want this now." The fool!

"She insisted," Silkowitz said, and slid away. He looked afraid; for the first time he looked respectful. Matt felt his own force; his howl was already in his throat. What was Frances up to? Transgression, invasion!

He read: "metamerism," "oribi," "glyptic," "enatic"—all in Frances's compact, orderly fountain-pen print. But an inch below, in rapid pencil: *Be advised. I saw him. He's here.*

She had chosen her seat herself: front row balcony, an aerie from which to spot the reviewers and eavesdrop on the murmurs, the sighs, the whispers. She meant to spy, to search out who was and wasn't there. Aha: then Lionel was there. He was in the audience. He had turned up after all—out of rivalry. Out of jealousy. Because of the buzz. To get the lay of Silkowitz's land. An old director looking in on a young one: age, fear, displacement. They were saying Lionel was past it; they were saying little Teddy Silkowitz, working on a shoestring out of a dinky cell over a sex shop, was cutting edge. So Lionel was out there, Lionel who made Matt audition, who humiliated him, who stuck him with the geezer role, a bit part in the last scene of a half-baked London import.

> As flies to wanton boys are we to the gods; they kill
> us for their sport.
> Unaccommodated man is no more but such a poor,
> bare, fork'd animal as thou art.

Lear on the heath—now let Lionel learn what a geezer role could be, and Matt in it!

Lionel wasn't out there. He would not come for Silkowitz, he would not come for Matt. Matt understood this. It was someone else Frances had seen.

He made his second-act entrance. The set was abstract, filled with those cloth-wrapped wooden free forms that signified the city. Silkowitz had brought the heath to upper Broadway. But no one laughed, no one coughed. It was Lear all the same, daughter-betrayed, in a storm, half mad, sported with by the gods, a poor, bare, forked animal, homeless, shoeless, crying in the gutters of a city street on a snowy night. The fake snow drifted down. Matt's throat let out its unholy howl; it spewed out old forgotten exiles, old lost cities, Constantinople, Alexandria, kingdoms abandoned, refugees ragged and driven, distant ash heaps, daughters unborn, Frances's wasted eggs and empty uterus, the wild roaring cannon of a human heartbeat.

A noise in the audience. Confusion; another noise. Matt moved downstage, blinded, and tried to peer through the lights. A black silhouette was thudding up the middle aisle, shrieking. Three stairs led upward to the apron; up thudded the silhouette. It was Eli Miller in a threadbare cape, waving a walking stick.

"This is not the way! This is not the way!" Eli Miller yelled, and slammed his stick down again and again on the floor of the stage. "Liars, thieves, corruption! In the mother tongue, with sincerity, not from such a charlatan like this!" He thudded toward Matt; his breath was close. It smelled of farina. Matt saw the one blue eye, the one dead eye.

"Jacob Adler, *he* could show you! Not like this! Take Eli Miller's word for it, this is not the way! You weren't there, you didn't see, you didn't hear!" With his old butcher's arm he raised his stick. "People," he called, "listen to Eli Miller, they're leading you by the nose here, it's charlatanism! Pollution! Nobody remembers! Ladies and gentlemen, my daughter, she wasn't born yet, mediocre! Eli Miller is telling you, this is not the way!"

Back he came to Matt. "You, you call yourself an actor? You with the rotten voice? Jacob Adler, this was a thunder, a rotten voice is not a thunder! Maurice Schwartz, the Yiddish Art Theater, right around the corner it used to be, there they did everything beautiful, Gordin, even Herzl once, Hirschbein, Leivick, Ibsen, Molière. Lear! And whoever was there, whoever saw Jacob Adler's Lear, what they saw was not of this earth!"

In a tide of laughter the audience stood up and clapped — a volcano of applause. The laughter surged. Silkowitz ran up on the stage and hauled the old man off, his cape dithering behind him, his stick in the air, crying Lear, Lear. Matt was still loitering there in his bare feet, watching the wavering cape and the bobbing stick, when the curtain fell and hid him in the dark. Many in the audience, Frances informed him later, laughed until they wept.

AT FUMICARO

Frank Castle knew everything. He was an art critic; he was a book critic; he wrote on politics and morals; he wrote on everything. He was a journalist, both in print and weekly on the radio; he had "sensibility," but he was proud of being "focused." He was a Catholic; he read Cardinal Newman and François Mauriac and Étienne Gilson and Simone Weil and Jacques Maritain and Graham Greene. He reread *The Heart of the Matter* a hundred times, weeping (Frank Castle could weep) for poor Scobie. He was a parochial man who kept himself inside a frame. He had few Protestant and no Jewish friends. He said he was interested in happiness, and that was why he liked being Catholic. Catholics made him happy.

Fumicaro made him happy. To get there he left New York on an Italian liner, the *Benito Mussolini.* Everything about it was talkative but excessively casual. The schedule itself was casual, and the ship's engines growled in the slip through a whole day before embarkation. Aboard, the passageways were packed with noisy promenaders — munchers of stuffed buns with their entrails dripping out (in all that chaos the dock peddlers had somehow pushed through), quaffers of colored fizzy waters.

At the train station in Milan he found a car, at an exorbitant rate, to take him to Fumicaro. He was already hours late. He was on his way to the Villa Garibaldi, established by a Chicago philanthropist who had set the place up for conferences of a virtuous nature. The Fascists interfered, but not much, out of a lazy sense of duty; so far, only a convention of lepidopterists had been sent away. One of the lepidopterists had been charged with supplying information, not about butterflies, to gangs of anti-Fascists in their hideouts in the hills around Fumicaro.

There were wonders all along the road: dun brick houses Frank Castle had thought peculiar only to certain neighborhoods in the Bronx, each with its distinctive four-sided roof and, in the dooryard of each, a fig tree tightly mummified in canvas. It was still November, but not cold, and the banks along the spiraling mountain route were rich with purple flowers. As they ascended, the driver began to hum a little, especially where the curves were most hair-raising, and when a second car came hurtling into sight from the opposite direction in a space that seemed too narrow even for one, Frank Castle believed death was near; and yet they passed safely and climbed higher. The mountain grew more and more decorous, sprouting antique topiary and far flecks of white villas.

In the Villa Garibaldi the three dozen men who were to be his colleagues were already at dinner, under silver chandeliers; there was no time for him to be taken to his room. The rumbling voices put him off a bit, but he was not altogether among strangers. He recognized some magazine acquaintances and three or four priests, one of them a public charmer whom he had interviewed on the radio. After the conference —it was called "The Church and How It Is Known," and

would run four days—almost everyone was planning to go
on to Rome. Frank Castle intended to travel to Florence first
(he hoped for a glimpse of the portrait of Thomas Aquinas
in the San Marco), and then to Rome, but on the fourth day,
entirely unexpectedly, he got married instead.

After dinner there was a sluggish session around the huge
conference board in the hall next to the dining room—Frank
Castle, who had arrived hungry, now felt overfed—and then
Mr. Wellborn, the American director, instructed one of the
staff (a quick hollow-faced fellow who had waited on Frank
Castle's table) to lead him down to the Little Annex, the cottage where he was to sleep. It was full night now; there was a
stone terrace to cross, an iron staircase down, a pebbled path
weaving between lofty rows of hedges. Like the driver, the
waiter hummed, and Frank Castle looked to his footing. But
again there was no danger—only a strangeness, and a fragrance so alluring that his nostrils strained after it with appetite. The entrance to the Little Annex was an engaging low
archway. The waiter set down Frank Castle's suitcase on the
gravel under the arch, handed him a big cold key, and pointed
upward to a circular flight of steps. Then he went humming
away.

At the top of the stairs Frank Castle saw a green door, but
there was no need for the key—the door was open; the lamp
was on. Disorder; the bed unmade, though clean sheets were
piled on a chair. An empty wardrobe; a desk without a telephone; a bedside cabinet, holding the lit gooseneck; a loud
clock and a flashlight; the crash of water in crisis. It was the
sound of a toilet flushing again and again. The door to the
toilet gaped. He went in and found the chambermaid on her
knees before it, retching; in four days she would be his wife.

He was still rather a young man, yet not so young that he
was unequal to suddenness. He was thirty-five, and much of

his life had flowered out of suddenness. He did not know exactly what to do, but he seized a washcloth, moistened it with cold water at the sink, and pressed it against the forehead of the kneeling woman. She shook it off with an animal sound.

He sat on the rim of the bathtub and watched her. He did not feel especially sympathetic, but he did not feel disgust either. It was as if he were watching a waterfall—a thing belonging to nature. Only the odor was unnatural. Now and then she turned her head and threw him a wild look. *Condemn what thou art, that thou mayest deserve to be what thou art not*, he said to himself; it was Saint Augustine. It seemed right to him to think of that just then. The woman went on vomiting. A spurt of colorless acrid liquid rushed from her mouth. Watching serenely, he thought of some grand fountain where dolphins, or else infant cherubim, spew foamy white water from their bottomless throats. He saw her shamelessly: she was a solid little nymph. She was the coarse muse of Italia. He recited to himself, *If to any man the tumult of the flesh were silenced, silenced the phantasies of earth, waters, and air, silenced, too, the poles.*

She reached back with one hand and grasped the braid that lay along her neck. Her nape, bared, was running with sweat, and also with tears that trailed from the side of her mouth and around. It was a short robust neck, like the stem of a mushroom.

"Are you over it?" he said.

She lifted her knees from the floor and sat back on her heels. Now that she had backed away from it, he could see the shape of the toilet bowl. It was, to his eyes, foreign-looking: high, much taller than the American variety, narrow. The porcelain lid, propped upright, was bright as a mirror. The rag she had been scrubbing it with was lost in her skirt.

Now she began to hiccup.

"Is it over?"

She leaned her forehead along the base of the washstand. The light was not good — it had to travel all the way from the lamp on the table in the bedchamber and through the door, dimming as it came; nevertheless her color seemed high. Surely her lips were swollen; they could not have been intended to bulge like that. He believed he understood just how such a face ought to have been composed. With her head at rest on the white pillar of the sink, she appeared to him (he said these words to himself slowly and meticulously, so clarified and prolonged was the moment for him) like an angel seen against the alabaster column that upholds the firmament. Her hiccups were loud, frequent; her shoulders jerked, and still the angel did not fall.

She said, *"Le dispiace se mi siedo qui? Sono molto stanca."*

The pointless syllables — it was his first day in Italy — made him conscious of his stony stare. His own head felt stone: was she a Medusa? — those long serpents of her spew. It occurred to him that, having commenced peacefully enough, he was far less peaceful now. He was, in fact, staring with all his might, like a statue, a stare without definition or attachment, and that was foolish. There was a glass on the shelf over the sink. He stood up and stepped over her feet (the sensation of himself as great arch-of-triumph darkening her body) and filled the glass with water from the tap and gave it to her.

She drank as quickly as a child, absorbed. He could hear her throat race and shut on its hinge, and race again. When the glass was empty she said, *"Molto gentile da parte sua. Mi sento così da ieri. È solo un piccolo problema."* All at once she saw how it was for him: he was a foreigner and could not understand. Recognition put a smoke of anxiety over her eyes. She said loudly, *"Scusi,"* and lapsed into a brevity of English as peculiar as any he had ever heard, surprising in that it was there at all: "No belief!" She jumped up on her thick legs and let her braid hang. *"Ho vomitato!"* she called — a war cry roughened by victorious good humor. The rag separated itself from the folds of her big skirt and slid to the floor, and just then, while he was contemplating the density of her calves and the wonder of their roundness and heaviness, she seemed as he watched to grow lighter and lighter, to escape from the rough aspiring weight that had pulled her up, and she fell like a rag, without a noise.

Her lids had slapped down. He lifted her and carried her — heaved her — onto the bed and felt for her pulse. She was alive. He had never before been close to a fainted person. If he had not seen for himself how in an instant she had shut herself off, like a faucet turned, he would have been certain that the woman he had set down on the naked gray mattress was asleep.

The night window was no better than a blind drawn to: no sight, no breath, no help. Only the sweet grassy smells of the dark mountainside. He ran halfway down the spiral stone staircase and then thought, Suppose, while I am gone, the woman dies. She was only the chambermaid; she was a sound girl, her cheeks vigorous and plump; he knew she would not die. He locked the door and lay down beside her in the lamplight, riding his little finger up and down her temple. It was a marvel and a luxury to be stretched out there with her, unafraid. He assured himself she would wake and not die.

He was in a spiritual condition. He had been chaste for almost six months — demandingly pure, even when alone, even inside his secret mind. His mind was a secret cave, immaculately swept and spare. It was an initiation. He was preparing himself for the first stages of a kind of monasticism. He did not mean that he would go off and become a monk in a monastery: he knew how he was of the world. But he intended to be set apart in his own privacy: to be strong and transcendent, above the body. He did not hope to grow into a saint, yet he wanted to be more than ordinary, even while being counted as "normal." He wanted to possess himself first, so that he could yield himself, of his own accord, to the forces of the spirit.

Now here was his temptation. It seemed right — foreordained — that he would come to Italy to be lured and tempted. The small rapture versus the greater rapture — the rapture in the body and the rapture in God, and he was for the immensity. Who would not choose an ocean, with its heaven-tugged tides, over a single drop? He looked down at the woman's face and saw two wet black drops, each one an opened eye.

"Do you feel sick again? Are you all right?" he said, and took away his little finger.

"No belief! No belief!"

The terrible words, in her exhausted croak, stirred him to the beginning of a fury. What he had done, what he had endured, to be able to come at last to belief! And a chambermaid, a cleaner of toilets, could cry so freely against it!

He knew her meaning: she was abashed, shame punched out her tears, she was sunk in absurdity and riddle. But still it shook him — he turned against her — because every day of his life he had to make this same pilgrimage to belief all over again, starting out each dawn with the hard crow's call of no belief.

"No belief! No belief!" she croaked at him.

"Stop that."

She raised herself on her wrist, her arm a bent pole. "Signore, *mi scusi,* I make the room —"

"Stay where you are."

She gestured at the pile of sheets on the chair, and fell back again.

"Do they know you're sick? Does Mr. Wellborn know?"

She said laboriously, "I am two day sick." She touched her stomach and hiccupped. "I am no sick two day like now."

He could not tell from this whether she meant she was better or worse. "Do you want more water?"

"Signore, *grazie,* no water."

"Where do you stay?" He did not ask where she lived; he could not imagine that she lived anywhere.

Her look, still wet, trailed to the window. "In the town."

"That's all the way down that long road I drove up."

"*Sì.*"

He reflected. "Do you always work so late?"

"Signore, in this morning when I am sick I no make the room, I come back to make finish the room. I make finish all the room"—her eyes jumped in the direction of the Villa —"only the signore's room I no make."

He let out his breath: a wind so much from the well of his ribs that it astonished him. "They don't know where you are." He was in awe of his own lung. "You can stay here," he said.

"Oh, Signore, *grazie,* no —"

"Stay," he said, and elevated his little finger. Slowly, slowly, he dragged it across her forehead. A late breeze, heavy with the lazy fragrance of some alien night bloomer, had cooled her. He tasted no heat in the tiny salted cavern between her nose and her mouth. The open window brought him the smell of water; during the taxi's climb to the Villa Garibaldi he had scarcely permitted himself a glimpse of old shining Como, but now his nostrils were free and full: he took in the breath of the lake while again letting out his own. He unbuttoned his shirt and wiped every cranny of her face with it, even inside her ears; he wiped her mushroom neck. He had worn this shirt all the way from Leghorn, where the *Benito Mussolini* had docked, to Milan, and from the train station in

Milan to Fumicaro. He had worn it for twenty hours. By now it was dense with the exhalations of Italy, the sweat of Milan.

When he spoke of Milan she pushed away his shirt. Her mother, she told him, lived in Milan. She was a maid at the Hotel Duomo, across from the cathedral. Everyone called her Caterina, though it wasn't her name. It was the name of the previous maid, the one who got married and went away. They were like that in Milan. They treated the maids like that. The Duomo was a tourist hotel; there were many Americans and English; her mother was quick with foreign noises. Her mother's English was very good, very quick; she claimed to have learned it out of a book. An American had given her a bilingual dictionary to keep, as a sort of tip.

In Milan they were not kind. They were so far north they were almost like Germans or Swiss. They cooked like the Swiss, and they had cold hearts like the Germans. Even the priests were cold. They said ordinary words so strangely; they accused Caterina of a mischief called "dialect," but the mischief was theirs, not hers. Caterina had a daughter, whom she had left behind in Calabria. The daughter lived with Caterina's old mother, but when the daughter was thirteen Caterina had summoned her north to Milan, to work in the hotel. The daughter's name was Viviana Teresa Accenno, and it was she who now lay disbelieving in Frank Castle's bed in the Little Annex of the Villa Garibaldi. Viviana at thirteen was very small, and looked no more than nine or ten. The manager of the Duomo did not wish to employ her at all, but Caterina importuned, so he put the girl into the kitchen to help with the under-chefs. She washed celery and broccoli; she washed the grit out of the spinach and lettuce. She reached with the scrub brush under the stove and behind it, crevices where no one else could fit. Her arm then was a little stick for poking.

Unlike Caterina, she hardly ever saw any Americans or English. Despite the bilingual dictionary, Viviana did not think that her mother could read anything at all—it was only that Caterina's tongue was so quick. Caterina kept the dictionary at the bottom of her wardrobe; sometimes she picked it up and cradled it, but she never looked into it. Still, her English was very fine, and she tried to teach it to Viviana. Viviana could make herself understood, she could say what she had to, but she could never speak English like Caterina.

Because of her good English Caterina became friends with the tourists. They gave her presents—silk scarves, and boxes made of olivewood, with celluloid crucifixes resting on velveteen inside, all the useless things tourists are attracted to—and in return she took parties out in the evenings; often they gave her money. She led them to out-of-the-way restaurants in neighborhoods they would never have found on their own, and to a clever young cobbler she was acquainted with, who worked in a shoe factory by day but measured privately for shoes at night. He would cut the leather on a Monday and have new shoes ready on a Wednesday—the most up-to-date fashions for the ladies, and for the gentlemen oxfords as sober and sturdy as anyone could wish. His prices were as low as his workmanship was splendid. The tourists all supposed he stole the leather from the factory, but Caterina guaranteed his probity and assured them this could not be. His jacket pockets were heavy with bits of leather of many shapes, and also straps and buckles, and tiny corked flacons of dye.

Caterina had all these ways of pleasing tourists, but she would not allow Viviana to learn any of them. Every Easter she made Viviana go back to spend a whole week with the grandmother in Calabria, and when Viviana returned, Caterina had a new Easter husband. She had always had a separate Milan husband, even when her Calabria husband, Viviana's father, was alive. It was not bigamy, not only because Caterina's Calabria husband had died long ago but also because Caterina had never, strictly speaking, been married in the regular way to the Milan husband. It wasn't that Caterina did not respect the priests; each day she went across the street and over the plaza to the cathedral to kneel in the nave, as broad as a sunless grassless meadow. The floor was made holy by the bones of a saint shut up in a box in front of the altar. All the priests knew her, and tried to persuade her to marry the Easter husband, and she always promised that very soon she would. And they in turn promised her a shortcut: if only she showed good will and an honest faith, she could become a decent wife overnight.

But she did not, and Viviana at length understood why: the Easter husband kept changing heads. Sometimes he had one head, sometimes another, sometimes again the first. You could not marry a husband who wore a different head all the time. Except for the heads, the Easter husband was uniformly very thin, from his Adam's apple all the way down to his fancy boots. One Easter he wore the cobbler's head, but Caterina threw him out. She said he was a thief. A silver crucifix she had received as a present from a Scottish minister was missing from the bottom of the wardrobe, though the bilingual dictionary was still there. But the cobbler came back with the news that he had a cousin in Fumicaro, where they were looking for maids for the American villa there; so Caterina decided to send her daughter, who was by now sixteen and putting flesh on her buttocks. For an innocent, Caterina said, the money was safer than in Milan.

And just then the grandmother died; so Caterina and Viviana and the cobbler all traveled down to Calabria for the funeral. That night, in the grandmother's tiny house, Viviana had a peculiar adventure, though as natural as rain; it only felt peculiar because it had never happened before — she had always trusted that someday it would. The cobbler and Caterina were crumpled up together in the grandmother's shabby bed; Caterina was awake, sobbing: she explained how she was a dog loose in the gutters, she belonged nowhere, she was a woman without a place, first a widow, now an orphan and the mother of an orphan. The highfaluting priests in the cathedral could not understand how it was for a widow of long standing. If a widow of long standing, a woman used to making her own way, becomes a wife, they will not allow her to make her own way anymore, she will be poorer as a poor man's wife than as a widow. What can priests, those empty pots, those eunuchs, know of the true life of a poor woman? Lamenting, Caterina fell asleep, without intending to, and then the cobbler with his bony shadow slipped out from the grandmother's bed and circled to the corner where Viviana slept, though now she was as wide awake as could be, in her cot near the stove, a cot dressed up during the day with a rosy fringed spread and crocheted cushions patterned with butterflies. The grandmother had let Viviana hug the pretty cushions at night, as if they were stuffed dolls. Viviana's lids were tight. She imagined that the saint's bones had risen from their northern altar and were sliding toward her in the dark. Caterina kept on clamorously breathing through the tunnel of her throat, and Viviana squeezed her shut eyes down on the butterflies. If she pressed them for minutes at a time, their wings would appear to flutter. She could make their wings stir just by pressing down on them. It seemed she was making the cobbler shudder now as he moved, in just that same way; her will was surely against it, and yet he was shuddering close to the cot. He had his undershirt on, and his bony-faced smile, and he shivered, though it was only September and the cabbage-headed trees in her grandmother's yard were luxuriant in the Calabrian warmth.

After this she came to Fumicaro to work as a chamber-maid at the Villa Garibaldi; she hadn't told her mother a thing about where the cobbler had put his legs and his arms, and not only because he had shown her the heavy metal of his belt. The cobbler was not to blame; it was her mother's mourning that was at fault, because if Caterina had not worn herself out with mourning the cobbler would have done his husband business in the regular way, with Caterina; and in-stead he had to do it with Viviana. All men have to do hus-band business, even if they are not regular husbands; it is how men are. How you are also, Signore, an American, a tourist.

It was true. In less than two hours Frank Castle had become the lover of a child. He had carried her into his bed and coaxed her story from her, beginning with his little finger's trip across her forehead. Then he had let his little finger go riding else-where, riding and riding, until her sweat returned, and he be-gan to sweat himself; the black night window was not feeding them enough air. Air! It was like trying to breathe through a straw. He drew the key from the door and steered her, both of them barefoot, down the curling stairs, and walked with her out onto the gravel, through the arch. There was no moon, only a sort of gliding whitish mist low to the ground, and transitory; sometimes it was there, sometimes not. At the foot of the invisible hill, below the long hairy slope of mountain-side, Como stretched like a bit of black silk nailed down. A galaxy prickled overhead, though maybe not: lights of villas high up, chips of stars — in such a blackness it was impossible to know the difference. She pointed far out, to the other side of the lake: nothingness. Yet there, she said, stood the pinkish palace of Il Duce, filled with seventy-five Fascist servants, and a hundred soldiers who never slept.

· · ·

After breakfast, at the first meeting of the morning, a young priest read a paper. It seemed he had forgotten the point of the conference — public relations — and was speaking devoutly, illogically. His subject was purity. The flesh, he said, is holy bread, like the shewbread of the Israelites, meant to be consecrated for God. To put it to use for human pleasure alone is defilement. The words inflamed Frank Castle: he had told Viviana to save his room for last and to wait for him there in the afternoon. At four o'clock, after the day's third session, while the others went down the mountain — the members had been promised a ride across Como in a motor launch — he climbed to the green door of the Little Annex and once again took the child into his bed.

He knew he was inflamed. He felt his reason had been undermined, like a crazy man's. He could not get enough of this woman, this baby. She came to him again after dinner; then he had to attend the night session, until ten; then she was in his bed again. She was perfectly well. He asked her about the nausea. She said it was gone, except very lightly, earlier that day; she was restored. He could not understand why she was yielding to him this way. She did whatever he told her to. She was only afraid of meeting Guido, Mr. Wellborn's assistant, on her way to the Little Annex: Guido was the one who kept track of which rooms were finished, and which remained, and in what order. Her job was to make the beds and change the towels and clean the floors and the tub. Guido said the Little Annex must be done first. It was easy for her to leave the Little Annex for last — it had only two rooms in it, and the other was empty. The person who was to occupy the empty room had not yet arrived. He had sent no letter or telegram. Guido had instructed Viviana to tend to the empty room all the same, in case he should suddenly make his appearance. Mr. Wellborn was still expecting him, whoever it was.

On the third day, directly after lunch, it was Frank Castle's turn to speak. He was, after all, he said, only a journalist. His paper would be primarily neither theological nor philosophical — on the contrary, it was no more than a summary of a series of radio interviews he had conducted with new converts. He would attempt, he said, to give a collective portrait of these. If there was one feature they all had in common, it was what Jacques Maritain named as "the impression that evil was truly and substantially someone." To put it otherwise, these were men and women who had caught sight of demons. Let us not suppose, Frank Castle said, that — at the start — it is the love of Christ that brings souls into the embrace of Christ. It is fear; sin; evil; true cognizance of the Opposer. The corridor to Christ is at bottom the Devil, just as Judas was the necessary corridor to redemption.

He read for thirty minutes, finished to a mainly barren room, and thought he had been too metaphorical; he should have tried more for the psychological — these were modern men. They all lived, even the priests, along the skin of the world. They had cleared out, he guessed, in order to walk down the mountain into the town in the brightness of midday. There was a hot chocolate shop, with pastry and picture postcards of Fumicaro: clusters of red tiled roofs, and behind them, like distant ice cream cones, the Alps — you could have your feet in Italy and your gaze far into Switzerland. Around the corner from the hot chocolate place, he heard them say, there was a little box of a shop, with a tinkling bell, easily overlooked if you didn't know about it. It was down an alley as narrow as a thread. You could buy leather wallets, and ladies' pocketbooks, also of leather, and shawls and neckties labeled *seta pura*. But the true reason his colleagues were drawn down to the town was to stand at the edge of Como. Glorious disc of lake! It had beckoned them yesterday. It beckoned today.

It summoned eternally. The bliss of its flat sun-shot surface; as dazzling as some huge coin. The room had emptied out toward it; he was not offended, not even discontent. He had not come to Fumicaro to show how clever he could be (nearly all these fellows were clever), or how devout; he knew he was not devout enough. And not to discover new renunciations, and not to catch the hooks the others let fly. And not even to be tested. He was beyond these trials. He had fallen not into temptation but into happiness. Happy, happy Fumicaro! He had, he saw, been led to Fumicaro not for the Church — or not directly for the Church, as the conference brochure promised — but for the explicit salvation of one needful soul.

She was again waiting for him. He was drilled through by twin powers: the power of joy, the power of power. She was obedient, she was his own small nun. The roundness of her calves made him think of loaves of round bread, bread like domes. She asked him — it was in a way remarkable — whether his talk had been a success. His "talk." A "success." She was alert, shrewd. It was clear she had a good brain. Already she was catching on. Her mind skipped, it was not static; it was a sort of burr that attached itself to whatever passed. He told her that his paper had not been found interesting. His listeners had drifted off to look at Como. Instantly she wanted to take him there — not through the town, with its lures for tourists, but down an old stone road, mostly overgrown, back behind the Villa Garibaldi, to the lake's unfrequented rim. She had learned about it from some of the kitchen staff. He was willing, but not yet. He considered who he was; where he was. A man on fire. He asked her once more if she was well. Only a little in the morning not, she said. He was not surprised; he was prepared for it. She had missed, she said, three bleedings. She believed she might be carrying the cobbler's seed, though she had washed herself and washed herself. She had cleaned out her insides until she was as dry as a saint.

She lay with her head against his neck. Her profile was very sharp. He had seen her head a hundred times before, in museums: the painted walls of Roman villas. The oversized eyes with their black oval shine, the nose broad but so splendidly symmetrical, the top lip with its two delectably lifted points. Nevertheless she was mysteriously not handsome. It was because of her caste. She was a peasant's child. Her skin was tawny — as if a perpetual brown shadow had dropped close against it, partly translucent. A dark lens stretched over her cheeks, through which he saw, minutely, the clarity of her youth. He thought she was too obedient; she had no pride. Meekness separated her from beauty. She urged her mouth on his neck and counted: *Settembre, Ottobre, Novembre,* all without the bleeding.

He began to explain the beginning of his plan: in a week or two she would see New York.

"New York! No belief!" She laughed — and there was her gold tooth! — and he laughed too, because of his idiocy, his recklessness; he laughed because he had really lost his reason now and was giving himself over to holy belief. She had been disclosed to him, and on her knees; it followed that he had been sent. Her laughter was all youth and clarity and relief — what she had escaped! Deliverance. His was clownishness: he was a shaman. And recognition: he was a madman, driven like a madman, or an idiot.

"You're all right," he said. "You'll be all right."

She went on laughing. "No belief! No belief! *Dio, Dio!*" She laughed out the comedy of her entanglements: a girl like herself, who had no husband, and goes three bleedings without bleeding, will be, she said, "finish" — she had seized the idiom out of the air. There was no place for her but the ditch. There would never be a regular husband for her — not in Fumicaro, not in Milano, not at home in Calabria, not anywhere on any piece of God's earth inhabited by the human family. No one would touch her. They would throw her in the ditch. She was in hell. Finish. God had commanded the American signore to pull her out from the furnace of hell.

He explained again, slowly (he was explaining it to himself), in a slow voice, with the plainest words he could muster, that he would marry her and take her home with him to America. To New York.

"New York!" She *did* believe him; she believed him on the instant. Her trust was electric. The beating of her belief entered his rib cage, thrashing and plunging its beak into his spine. He could not help himself: he was his own prisoner, he was inside his own ribs, pecking there. "New York!" she said. For this she had prayed to the Holy Bambino. Oh, not for New York, she had never prayed for America, who could dream it!

No belief: he would chain himself to a rock and be flung into the sea, in order to drown unbelief.

Therefore he would marry Viviana Teresa Accenno. It was his obeisance. It was what had brought him to Italy; it was what had brought him to the Little Annex of the Villa Garibaldi. There were scores of poor young women all over Italy — perhaps in Fumicaro itself — in her position. He could not marry them all. Her tragedy was a commonplace. She was a noisy aria in an eternal opera. It did not matter. This girl was the one he had been led to. Now the power traveled from him to her; he felt the pounding of her gratitude, how it fed her, how it punished him, how she widened herself for him, how stalwart she was, how nervy! He was in her grip, she was his slave; she had the vitality of surrender. For a few moments it made her his master.

He did not return to the salons and chandeliers of the Villa Garibaldi that day — not for the pre-dinner session or for the after-dinner session; and not for dinner either. From then on everything went like quicksilver. Viviana ran to find Guido, to report that she was short of floor wax; he gave her the key to the supply closet, which was also the wine cellar. Easeful Fumicaro! where such juxtapositions reigned. She plucked a flask of each: wax and wine. Mr. Wellborn blinked at such pilfering; it kept the staff content. It was only Guido who was harsh. Still, it was nothing at all for her to slip into the kitchen and spirit away a fat fresh bread and a round brick of cheese. They trod on ivy that covered the path under the windows of the grand high room that held the meadow-long conference board. Frank Castle could hear the cadenced soughing of the afternoon speaker. The sun was low but steady. She took him past enormous bricked-up arches, as tall as city apartment buildings. In the kitchen, where they were so gullible, they called it the Roman aqueduct, but nobody sensible supposed that Romans had once lived here. It was *stupido,* a tale for children. They say about the Romans that they did not have God; the priests would not let them linger in holy Italy if they did not know Jesus, so they must have lived elsewhere. She did not doubt that they had once existed, the Romans, but elsewhere. In Germany, maybe in Switzerland. Only never in Italy. The Pope of those days would never have allowed infidels to stay in such a place as Fumicaro. Maybe in Naples! Far down, under their feet, they could descry a tiny needle: it was the bell tower of the ancient church in Fumicaro. Frank Castle had already inquired about this needle. It had been put there in the twelfth century. Wild irises obscured the stone road; it wound down and down, and was so spare and uneven that they had to go single file. They met no one. It was all theirs. He had a sense of wingedness: how quickly they came to the lip of Como. The lake was all gold. A sun-ball was submerged in it as still as the yolk of an egg, and the red egg on the horizon also did not move. They encamped in a wilderness — thorny bushes and a jumble of long-necked, thick-speared grasses.

The wine was the color of light, immaculately clear, and warm, and wonderfully sour. He had never before rejoiced in such a depth of sourness — after you swallowed some and contemplated it, you entered the second chamber of the sourness, and here it was suddenly applelike. Their mouths burst into orchards. They were not hungry; they never broke off even a crumb of the bread and cheese; of these they would make a midnight supper, and in the early morning they would pay something to the milk driver, who would carry them as far as he could. The rest of the trip they would go by bus, like ordinary people. Oh, they were not ordinary! And in Milan Viviana would tell Caterina everything — everything except where the cobbler had put his legs and his arms; she would not mention the cobbler at all — and Caterina would lead them across the plaza into the cathedral, and the priests would marry them in the shortcut way they had always promised to Caterina and her Easter husband.

It was nearly night. Como had eaten the red egg; it was gone. Streaks of white and pink trailed over water and sky. There was still enough light for each to see the other's face. They passed the bottle of wine between them, back and forth, from hand to hand, stumbling upward, now and then wandering wide of the path — the stones were sometimes buried. A small abandoned shrine blocked the way. The head was eroded, the nose chipped. "This must be a Roman road," he told her. "The Romans built it."

"No belief!" It was becoming their life's motto.

The air felt miraculously dense, odorous with lake and bush. It could almost be sucked in, it was so liquidly thick. They spiraled higher, driving back the whiplike growth that snapped at their eyes. She could not stop laughing, and that made him start again. He knew he was besotted.

Directly in front of them the grasses appeared to part. Noises; rustle and flutter and an odd abrasive sound — there was no mistake, the bushes were moving. The noises ran ahead with every step they took; the disturbance in the bushes and the growling scrape were always just ahead. He thought of the malcontents who were said to have their hiding places in the mountains — thugs; he thought of the small mountain beasts that might scramble about in such a place — a fox? He was perfectly ignorant of the usual habitat of foxes. Then — in what was left of the dusk — he caught sight of a silhouette considerably bigger and less animate than a fox. It was a squarish thing kicking against the vegetation and scudding on the stones. It looked to be attached to a pallid human shape, broad but without glimmer, also in silhouette.

"Hello?" said an elderly American voice. "Anybody back there speak English?"

"Hello," Frank Castle called.

The square thing was a suitcase.

"Damn cab let me off at the bottom. Said he wouldn't go up the hill in the dark. Didn't trust his brakes. Damn lazy thieving excuse — I paid him door to door. This can't be the regular way up anyhow."

"Are you headed for the Villa Garibaldi?"

"Three days late to boot. You mixed up in it? Oh, it just

stirs my blood when they name a bed to sleep in after a national hero."

"I'm mixed up in it. I came on the *Benito Mussolini*," Frank Castle said.

"Speaking of never getting a night's sleep. So did I. Didn't see you aboard. Didn't see anyone. Stuck to the bar. Not that I can see you now, getting pitch black. Don't know where the hell I am. Dragging this damn thing. Is that a kid with you? I'll pay him to lug my bag."

Frank Castle introduced himself, there on the angle of the mountainside, on the Roman road, in the tunneling night. He did not introduce Viviana. All his life it would be just like that. She crept back off the bit of path into the thornbushes.

"Percy Nightingale," the man said. "Thank you kindly but never mind, if the kid won't take it, I'll carry it myself. Damn lazy types. How come you're on the loose, they haven't corralled you for the speeches?"

"You've missed mine."

"Well, I don't like to get to these things too early. I can sum up all the better if I don't sit through too many speeches — I do a summing-up column for the *All-Parish Taper*. Kindles Brooklyn and Staten Island. What've I missed besides you?"

"Three days of inspiration."

"Got my inspiration in Milan, if you want the truth. Found a cheapo hotel with a bar and had myself a bender. Listen, if you get up to Milan again take a gander at the *Last Supper* — it's just about over. Peeling. I give it no more'n fifty years. And for God's sake don't skip that messed-up *Pietà* — half done, arms and legs in such a tangle you wouldn't believe. Extra legs stuck in. My God, what now?" They had come flat out against a wall.

Viviana jumped into the middle of the stone road and zigzagged leftward. An apparition of battlements: high box hedges. Without any warning they had emerged right under the iron staircase abutting the kitchen of the Villa Garibaldi.

Climbing, the man with the suitcase said, "The name's familiar. Haven't I heard you on the radio, WJZ, those interviews with convicts?"

"Converts."

"I know what I said."

Viviana had evaporated.

"Are you the one Mr. Wellborn's expecting?"

"Mister who?"

"Wellborn," Frank Castle said. "The director. You'd better go to his office first. I think we're going to be neighbors."

"Love thy neighbor as thyself. He doesn't sound like a Wop."

"He's a Presbyterian from New Jersey."

"Myself, I'm a specialist. Not that I ever got my degree. I specialize in Wops and Presbyterians. Ad hoc and à la carte. We all have to make a living."

In his cups, Frank Castle thought. Then he remembered that he was drunk himself. He dug into his pocket and said with patient annoyance, "You know you can still catch the night session if you want. Here, take my program. It lists the whole conference. They were handing these out after Mass on the first day."

Percy Nightingale said, "After Mass? Liturgy giving birth to jargon. The sublime giving birth to what you'd damn well better be late arriving at."

But it was too dark to read.

In the Little Annex, behind the green door, Frank Castle began to pack. The wine had worn off. He wondered whether his stupefying idea — his idiocy — would wear off. He tested his will: was it still firm? He had no will. He had no purpose.

He did not know what he was thinking. He was not thinking of a wedding. He felt infinitely bewildered. He stood staring at his shirts. Had Viviana run down the mountain again, into Fumicaro, to fetch her things from her room? They had not planned that part. Somehow he took it for granted that she had no possessions, or that her possessions did not matter, or were invisible. He saw that he had committed the sin of heroism, which always presumes that everyone else is unreal, especially the object of rescue. She was the instrument of his carnality, the occasion of his fall; no more than that, though that was too much. He had pushed too far. A stranger, a peasant's child. He was no more capable of her salvation than of his own.

The doorknob turned. He hardly understood what he would say to her. After all, she was a sort of prostitute, the daughter of a sort of prostitute. He did not know exactly what these women were — the epiphenomena, he supposed, of the gradual movement, all over the globe, of the agricultural classes to the city. He was getting his reason back again. She, on her side, was entirely reasonable. An entrapment. Such women are always looking for free tickets to the New World. She had planted herself in his room — just his luck — to pretend sickness. All right, she hadn't pretended; he could see it wasn't pretense. All the more blatant. A scheme; a pit; a noose. With her bit of English she had examined the conference lists and found her eligible prey: an unmarried man. The whole roster were married men — it was only the priests and himself. So she had done her little research. A sensible girl who goes after what she wants. He was willing to give her some money, though God was his witness he didn't have so much that he could take on an extended program of philanthropy — his magazine, the *Sacral Review,* was making good his expenses. All the same he had to pinch. It was plain to him that she had never expected him to redeem the impulse of his dementia. It was his relief — the relief he felt in coming to his senses — that she had all along meant to exploit. Relief and the return of sanity were what he had to pay for. Mild enough blackmail. He wrenched his head round.

There stood Nightingale, anxiously jubilating and terrifically white. He had, so far, been no more than an old man's voice in the night, and to the extent that a voice represents a soul, he had falsified, he had misrepresented utterly. He was no older than Frank Castle, and it was not only that he was alarmingly indistinct — his ears were blanched; his mouth was a pinkish line; his eyes, blue overrinsed to a transparency, were humps in a face as flat as zinc. He was almost blotted out. His look was a surprise: white down to his shoes, and immensely diffident. His shirt was white, his thighs were white, his shoes the same, and even shyer; he was self-effacing. He had already taken off his pants — he was without dazzle or glare. Washed out to a Celtic pallor. Frank Castle was unsure, with all this contradiction between words and appearance, where to put his confidence.

"You're right. Neighbors," Nightingale said. "You can have your program back. I've got the glory of my own now. It's a wonder *any*one shows up for these things. It puts the priests to sleep, not that you can tell the difference when they're awake. I don't mind myself forgoing the pleasure" — he shook open the little pamphlet — "of, get this, 'Approaches to Bigotry.' 'The Church and the Community, North, East, South, West.' 'The Dioceses of Savannah, Georgia, and Denver, Colorado, Compared.' 'Parish or Perish . . .' My God, I wish I could go to bed."

"No one's forcing you to attend," Frank Castle said.

"You bet they're not. If I sum up better by turning up late, I sum up best if I don't turn up at all. Listen, I like a weight on me when I sleep. No matter what the climate or the weather, put me in the tropics, I've got to have plenty of blankets. I told them so in the office—they're sending the chambermaid. Not that she isn't taking her own sweet time. No wonder, godforsaken place they've stuck us in, way down here. The rest get to sleep like princes in the palace. I know about me, I always get the short straw, but what's your crime, you're not up at the big house? . . . Hey, you packing?"

Was he really packing? There were his shirts in a mound, folded and waiting to be folded, and his camera; there was his open suitcase.

"Not that I blame you, running off. Three days of it should do anyone." Nightingale tossed the pamphlet on the bed. "You've paid your dues. Especially if you got to stick in your two cents with the speechifying—what on?"

Footsteps on the circling stairs. Heavy goat steps. Viviana, obscured by blankets. She did not so much as glance in.

"Interviews with convicts," Frank Castle said.

Nightingale guffawed—the pouncing syllables of a hawk, the thread of the lips drawn covertly in. A hider. Recklessness at war with panic. Mistrusting the one, Frank Castle believed in the other. Panic. "What's your fix on these fellows? Cradle Catholics in my family since Adam, if not before, but I got my catechism from Father Leopold Robin."

"Never heard of him."

"Wouldn't expect you to. *Né* Rabinowitz."

Frank Castle felt himself heat up. The faintest rise of vertigo. It was stupid to give in to peculiar sensations just because Viviana hadn't looked in the door. He said, "Would you mind asking the chambermaid"—the word tugged at his tongue, as if it had fallen into something glutinous—"to stop by when she's finished at your place? They haven't changed my towels—"

"A whole speech on seeing the light? That's what you did? Too pious for me."

"Scientific. I put in the statistics. Enough to please even a specialist. How many converts per parish, what kinds of converts, from what kinds of backgrounds."

But he was listening to the small sounds in the next room.

Nightingale said, "Clare Boothe Luce. There's your trophy."

"We get all sorts these days. Because of the ascent of the Devil. Everyone's scared of the Devil. The rich and the poor. The soft and the arrogant—"

"And who's the Devil? You one of these fellows think Adolf's the new Satan? At least he holds off against the Commies."

"I'm willing to think you're the Devil," Frank Castle said.

"You're the touchy one."

"Well, a bit of the Devil's in all of us."

"Touchy and pious—I told you pious. Now you wouldn't think it would take a year to drop two blankets on a bed! All right, I'll send you that girl." He took two steps into the corridor and turned back. "This Father Robin wore the biggest crucifix you ever saw. Maybe it only looked big—I was just a kid. But that's how it is with these convicts—they're self-condemned, so they take their punishment more seriously than anybody. It gives me the willies when they come in hotter'n Hades. They act like a bunch of Holy Rollers with lights in their sockets. Show me a convert, I'll show you a fellow out to get even with someone. They're killers."

"Killers?"

"They kill the old self for the sake of the new self. Conversion," Nightingale said, "is revenge."

"You're forgetting Christ."

"Oh Jesus God. I never forget Christ. Why else would I

end up in this goddamn shack in this godforsaken country? Maybe the Fascists'll make something out of these Wops yet. Put some spine in 'em. You want that girl? I'll get you that girl."

Left to himself, Frank Castle dropped his head into his hands. With his eyes shut, staring into the flesh of the lids, he could see a whirligig of gold flecks. He had met a man and instantly despised him. It seemed to him that everyone here, not counting the handful of priests, was a sham — mountebanks all. And, for that matter, the priests as well. Publicrelations types. Journalists, editors. In an older time these people would have swarmed around the marketplace selling indulgences and hawking pigs' hair.

The chambermaid came in. She was a fleshless uncomprehending spindly woman of about forty, perspiring at the neck, with ankles like balloons. There was a purple mark in the middle of her left cheek. "Signore?" she said.

He went into the toilet and brought out a pair of fresh bath towels. "I won't need these. I'm leaving. You might as well do whatever you want with them."

She shook her head and backed away. He had already taken it in that she would not be able to follow a word. And anyhow his charade made no sense. Still, she accepted the towels with a maddening docility; she was no different from Viviana. Any explanation, no explanation, was all the same to these creatures.

He said, "Where's the other maid who always comes?"

The woman stared.

"Viviana," he said.

"Ah! *L'altra cameriera.*"

"Where is she?"

With the towels stuck firmly under one armpit, she lifted

her shoulders and held out her palms; then shut the door smartly behind her. A desolation entered him. He decided to attend the night session.

The meadow-long conference board had grown slovenly. Notebooks, squashed paper balls, pencils without points, empty pitchers and dirty cups, an exhausted coffee urn, languid eyeglasses lying with their earpieces askew; here and there a leg thrown up on the table. Formality had vanished, decay was crawling through. The meeting was well under way; the speaker was citing Pascal. It was very like a chant — he had sharp tidy hand gestures, a grocer slicing cheese. "'Not only do we understand God only through Jesus Christ, but we understand ourselves only through Jesus Christ. We understand life and death only through Jesus Christ. Outside Jesus Christ we do not know what life is, nor death, nor God, nor ourselves.' These words do not compromise; they do not try to get along with those who are indifferent to them, or with those who would laugh at them. They are neither polite nor gentle. They take their stand, and their stand is eternal and absolute. Today the obligation of Catholic public relations is not simply to defend the Church, though there is plenty of that to be done as well. In America especially we live with certain shadows, yet here in the mountains and valleys of Fumicaro, in glorious Italy, the Church is a serene mother, and it is of course easy to forget that she is troubled elsewhere. Elsewhere she is defamed as the refuge of superstition. She is accused of unseemly political advantages. She is assaulted as a vessel of archaism and as an enemy of the scientific intelligence. She is pointed to as an institution whose whole raison d'être is the advance of clerical power. Alas, the Church in her true soul, wearing her heavenly garments, is not sufficiently understood or known.

"All this public distortion is real enough, but our obligation is even more fundamental than finding the right lens of clarification to set over the falsifying portrait. The need to defend the Church against the debasement of the ignorant or the bigoted is, how shall we call it, a mere ripple in the sacred river. Our task as opinion makers — and we should feel no shame over this phrase, with all its American candor, for are we not Americans at an American colloquy, though we sit here charmed by the antiquity of our surroundings? — our task, then, is to show the timelessness of our condition, the applicability of our objectifying vision even to flux, even to the immediate instant. We are to come with our banner inscribed Eternity, and demonstrate its pertinence in the short run; indeed, in the shortest run of all, the single life, the single moment. We must let flower the absolute in the concrete, in the actual rise and fall of existence. Our aim is transmutation, the sanctification of the profane."

It was impossible to listen; Nightingale was right. Frank Castle sank down into some interior chamber of mind. He was secretive; he knew this about himself. It was not that he had habits of concealment, or that, as people say, he kept his own counsel. It was instead something akin to sensation, an ache or a bump. Self-recognition. Every now and then he felt the jolt of who he was and what he had done. He was a man who had invented his own designations. He was undetermined. He was who he said he was. No one, nothing, least of all chance, had placed him. Like Augustine, he interpreted himself, and hotly. Oh, hotly. Whereas this glacial propagandist, reciting his noble text, bleating out "absolute" and "concrete" and "transmutation," had fallen into his given slot like a messenger from fate. Once fallen, fixed. Rooted. A stalactite.

Far behind the speaker, just past the lofty brass-framed doorway — a distance of several pastures, a whole countryside — a plump little figure glimmered. Viviana! There she was;

there she stood. You would need a telescope to bring her close. Even with his unaccoutered eye, Frank Castle noticed how nicely she was dressed. If he had forgotten that she might have possessions, here was something pleasant — though it was only a blouse and skirt. She was clutching an object, he could not make out what. The blouse had a bright blue ribbon at the neck, and long sleeves. It might have been the ribbon, or the downward flow of the sleeves, or even the skirt, red as paint, which hung lower than he was used to — there was a sudden propriety in her. The wonderful calves were hidden: those hot globes he had only that afternoon drawn wide apart. Her thighs, too, were as hot and heavy as corn bread. Across such a space her head, remote and even precarious, was weighted down, like the laden head of a sunflower. She was absorbed by the marble floor tiles of the Villa Garibaldi. She would not come near. She eclipsed herself. She was a bit of shifting reflection.

He wondered if he should wait the speaker out. Instead he got up — every step a crash — and circled the table's disheveled infinitude. No one else moved. He was a scandal. Under the chandelier the speaker stuck to his paper. Frank Castle had done the same the day before, when they had all walked out on him for a ride across Como. Now here he was deserting, the only one to decamp. It was almost ten o'clock at night; the whole crew of them had been up since eight. One had made a nest of his rounded arms and was carefully, sweetly, cradling his face down into it. Another was propped back with his mouth open, brazenly asleep, something between a wheeze and a snuffle puffing intermittently out.

In the hall outside he said, "You've changed your clothes."

"We go Milano!"

She was in earnest then. Her steady look, diverted downward, was patient, docile. He did not know what to make of her; but her voice was too high. He set an admonitory finger over his own mouth. "Where did you disappear to?"

"I go, I put"—he watched her labor after the words; excitement throttled her—"*fiore. Il santo!* To make *un buon viaggio.*"

He was clear enough about what a *santo* was. "A saint? Is there a saint here?"

"You see before, in the road. You see," she insisted. She held up a metal cylinder. It was the flashlight from his bedside cabinet in the Little Annex. "Signore, come."

"Do you have things? You're taking things?"

"*La mia borsa, una piccolo valigia.* I put in the signore's room."

They could not stand there whispering. He followed where she led. She took him down the mountainside again, along the same half-buried road, to a weedy stone stump. It was the smothered little shrine he had noticed earlier. It grew right up out of the middle of the path. The head, with its rotted nose, was no more than a smudge. Over it, as tall as his hipbone, a kind of stone umbrella, a shelter like an upside-down U, or a fragment of vertical bathtub, seemed to be turning into a mound of wild ivy. Spiking out of this dense net was the iris Viviana had stuck there.

"San Francesco!" she said; the kitchen staff had told her. Such hidden old saints were all over the hills of Fumicaro.

"No," Frank Castle said.

"*Molti santi.* You no belief? Signore, see! San Francesco."

She gave him the flashlight. In its white pool everything had a vivid glaze, like a puppet stage. He peered at the smudge. Goddess or god? Emperor's head, mounted like a milestone to mark out sovereignty? The chin was rubbed away. The torso had crumbled. It hardly looked holy. Depending on the weather, it might have been as old as a hundred years, or a thousand; two thousand. Only an archeologist could say. But he did not miss how the flashlight conjured up effulgence. A halo blazed. Viviana was on her knees in the scrub; she tugged him down. With his face in leaves he saw the eroded fragment of the base, and, half sunken, an obscure tracing, a single intact word: DELEGI. I chose; I singled out. Who chose, what or who was singled out? Antiquity alone did not enchant him: the disintegrating image of some local Roman politico or evanescent godlet. The mighty descend to powder and leave chalk on the fingertips.

Her eyes were shut; she was now as she had been in her small faint, perfectly ordered; but her voice was crowded with fierce little mutterings. She was at prayer.

"Viviana. This isn't a saint."

She stretched forward and kissed the worn-away mouth.

"You don't know *what* it is. It's some old pagan thing."

"San Francesco," she said.

"No."

She turned on him a smile almost wild. The thing in the road was hallowed. It had a power; she was in thrall to sticks and stones. "*Il santo,* he pray for us." In the halo of the flashlight her cheeks looked oiled and sleek and ripe for biting. She crushed her face down into the leaves beside his own — it was as if she read him and would consent to be bitten — and said again, "Francesco."

He had always presumed that sooner or later he would marry. He had spiritual ambition; yet he wanted to join himself to the great protoplasmic heave of human continuity. He meant to be fruitful: to couple, to procreate. He could not be continent; he could not sustain purity; he was not chaste. He had a terrible inquisitiveness; his fall with Viviana was proof enough. He loved the priests, with their parched lip-corners and glossy eyes, their enigmatic loins burning for God. But he

could not become like them; he was too fitful. He had no hu-
mility. Sometimes he thought he loved Augustine more than
God. *Imitatio Dei:* he had come to Christ because he was secretive, because Jesus lived, though hiddenly. Hence the glory
of the thousand statues that sought to make manifest the reticent Christ. Sculptors, like priests, are least of all secretive.

Often it had seemed to Frank Castle that, marriage being
so open a cell, there was no one for him to marry. Wives were
famous for needing explanations. He could not imagine being
married to a bookish sort — an "intellectual" — but also he
feared this more than anything. He feared a wife who could
talk and ask questions and analyze and inquire after his history. Sometimes he fancied himself married to a rubber doll
about his own size. She would serve him. They would have a
rubber child.

A coldness breathed from the ground. Already hoarfrost
was beginning to gather — a blurry veil over the broken head
in the upended tub.

He said, "Get up."

"Francesco."

"Viviana, let's go." But he hung back himself. She was a
child of simple intuitions, a kind of primitive. He saw how
primitive she was. She was not a rubber doll, but she would
keep clear of the precincts of his mind. This gladdened him.
He wondered how such a deficiency could make him so glad.

She said for the third time, "Francesco." He understood finally that she was speaking his name.

They spent the night in his room in the Little Annex. At six
the milk driver would be grinding down from the kitchen lot
past the arch of the Little Annex. They waited under a bright-
ening sunrise. The mist was fuming free of the mountainside;
they could see all the way down to Como. Quietly loitering

side by side with the peasant's child, again Frank Castle knew himself slowly churning into chaos: half an hour ago she had stretched to kiss his mouth exactly as she had stretched to kiss the mouth of the pagan thing fallen into the ground. He was mesmerized by the strangeness he had chosen for himself: a whole life of it. She was clinging to his hand like an innocent; her fingers were plaited into his. And then, out of the blue, as if struck by a whirlwind, they were not. She tore herself from him; his fingers were ripped raw; it seemed like a seizure of his own skin; he lost her. She had hurled herself out of sight. Frank Castle watched her run — she looked flung. She ran into the road and down the road and across, behind the high hedges, away from the bricked-up vaults of the Roman aqueduct.

Percy Nightingale was descending from those vaults. Under his open overcoat a pair of bare bluish-white knees paraded.

"Greetings," he called, "from a practiced insomniac. I've been examining the local dawn. They do their dawns very nicely in these parts, I'll give 'em that. What detritus we travelers gather as we move among the realms — here you are with two bags, and last night I'm sure I saw you with only one. You don't happen to have any extra booze in one of those?" He stamped vaguely round in an uneven try at a circle. "Who was that rabbit who fled into the bushes?"

"I think you scared it off," Frank Castle said.

"The very sight of me? It's true I'm not dressed for the day. I intend to pull on my pants in time for breakfast. You seem to be waiting for a train."

"For the milk driver."

"Aha. A slow getaway. You'd go quicker with the booze driver. I'd come along for kicks with the booze driver."

"The fact of the matter," Frank Castle said in his flattest

voice, "is that you've caught me eloping with the chamber-maid."

"What a nice idea. Satan, get thee behind me and give me a push. Long and happy years to you both. The scrawny thing with the pachyderm feet and the birthmark? She made up my bed very snugly—I'd say she's one of the Roman evidences they've got around here." He pointed his long chin upward toward the aqueduct. "Since you didn't invite me to the exhumation, I won't be expected to be invited to the wedding. Believe it or not, here's your truck."

Frank Castle picked up Viviana's bag and his own and walked out into the middle of the road, fluttering his green American bills; the driver halted.

"See you in the funny papers," Nightingale yelled.

He sat in the seat next to the driver's and turned his face to the road. It snaked left and then left again: any moment now a red-skirted girl would scuttle out from behind a dip in the foliage. He tried to tell this to the driver, but the man only chirped narrowly through his country teeth. The empty steel milk cans on the platform in the back of the truck jiggled and rattled; sometimes their flanks collided—a robust clang like cymbals. It struck him then that the abyss in his entrails was his in particular: it wasn't fright at being discovered and judged that had made her bolt, but practical inhibition—she was canny enough, she wasn't about to run off with a crazed person. Lust! He had come to his senses yesterday, though only temporarily; she had come to hers today, and in the nick of time. After which it occurred to him that he had better look in his wallet. Duped. She had robbed him and escaped. He dived into his pocket.

Instantly the driver's open palm was under his nose.

"I paid you. *Basta*, I gave you *basta*."

The truck wobbled perilously around a curve, but the hand stayed.

"Good God! Keep hold of the wheel, can't you? We'll go off the road!"

He shook out a flood of green bills onto the seat. Now he could not know how much she had robbed him of. He did not doubt she was a thief. She had stolen cheese from the kitchen and wine from a locked closet. He thought of his camera. It would not surprise him if she had bundled it off in a towel or in a pillowcase in the night. Thievery had been her motive from the beginning. Everything else was ruse, snare, distraction, flimflam; she was a sort of gypsy, with a hundred tricks. He would never see her again. He was relieved. The freakishness of the past three days stung him; he grieved. Never again this surrender to the inchoate; never again the abyss. A joke! He had almost eloped with the chambermaid. Damn that Nightingale!

They rattled — sounding now like a squad of carillons — into Fumicaro. Here was the promenade; here was the hot chocolate shop; here was the church with its bell tower; here was morning-dazzled Como — high and pure the light that rose from it. "Autobus," he commanded the driver. He had spilled enough green gold to command. The country teeth showed the bliss of the newly rich. He was let out at an odd little turn of gossipy street, which looked as if it had never in all its existence heard tell of an autobus; and here — "No belief!" — was Viviana, panting hard. She could not catch her breath, because of the spy. A spy had never figured in their fears, God knows! A confusion and a danger. The spy would be sure to inform Guido, and Guido would be sure to inform Mr. Wellborn, or, worse yet, the cobbler's cousin, who, as it happened, was Guido's cousin too, only from the other side of the family. And then they would not let her go. No, they would not! They would keep her until her trouble became visible and ruinous, and then they would throw her into the ditch. The spy was an untrustworthy man. He was the man they had met on the hill, who took her for a boy. He was the man in the empty room of the Little Annex. The other *cameriera* had told her that on top of all the extra blankets she had brought him he had put all the towels there were, and then, oh! he pulled down the curtains and piled them on top of the towels. And he stood before the other *cameriera* shamelessly, without his *pantaloni!* And so what could she do? She flew down the secret stone path, she flew right past San Francesco without stopping, to get to the autobus piazza before the milk driver.

Droplets of sweat erupted in a phalanx on her upper lip. She gave him the sour blink of an old woman; he glimpsed the Calabrian grandmother, weathered by the world's suspicions. "You think I no come?"

He would not tell her that he thought she had stolen.

"No belief!" Out tumbled her hot laugh, redolent of his bed in the Little Annex. "When *questo bambino* finish" — she pressed the cushion of her belly — "you make new *bambino*, O.K.?"

In Milan in the evening (his fourth in Italy), in a cramped cold chapel in the cathedral, within sight of the relic, they were married by a priest who was one of Caterina's special friends.

Caterina herself surprised him: she was dressed like a businesswoman. She wore a black felt hat with a substantial brim; she was substantial everywhere. Her head was set alertly on a neck that kept turning, as if wired to a generator; there was nothing she did not take in with her big powerful eyes. He perceived that she took *him* in, all in a gulp. Her arm shot out to smack Viviana, because Viviana, though she had intended never to tell about the cobbler, on her wedding day could not dissemble. The arm drew back. Caterina would not smack Viviana in front of a tourist, an American, on her wedding day. She was respectful. Still, it was a slander — the cobbler did not go putting seeds into the wombs of innocent girls. Twisting her neck, Caterina considered the American.

"Three days? You are friend of my Viviana three days, Signore?" She tapped her temple, and then made circles in the air with her forefinger. "For what you want to marry my Viviana if you no put the seed?"

He knew what a scoundrel he seemed. The question was terrifying; but it was not meant for him. They went at it, the mother and the daughter, weeping and shrieking, in incomprehensible cascades: it was an opera, extravagant with drama, in a language he could not fathom. All this took place in Caterina's room in the Hotel Duomo, around the corner from a linen closet as capaciously filled with shelves as a library; he sat in a chair face to face with the wardrobe in which the bilingual dictionary was secreted. The door was at his right hand — easy enough to grab the knob and walk away. For nearly an hour he sat. The two barking mouths went on barking. The hands clenched, grasped, pushed. He was detached, distant; then, to his amazement, at a moment of crescendo, when the clamor was at its angriest, the two women fell into a fevered embrace. Implausible as it was, preposterous as it was, Caterina was sending Viviana to America. *Un colpo di fulmine! Un fulmine a ciel sereno!*

Just before the little ceremony, the priest asked Frank Castle how he would feel about a child that was — as he claimed — not his. Frank Castle could not think what to say. The priest was old and exhausted. He spoke of sin as an elderly dog who is too sick to be companionable — yet you are used to him, you can't do without him, you can't bring yourself to get rid of him. The wedding ring was Caterina's.

Frank Castle exchanged his return ticket for two others on the *Stella Italiana,* sailing for New York in ten days. It was all accident and good luck: someone had canceled. There were two available places. That left time for the marriage to be accorded a civil status: the priest explained to Caterina that though in the eyes of God Viviana was now safe, they had to fetch a paper from the government and get it stamped. This was the law.

There was time for Milan. It was a curiosity: Viviana had been brought to this northern treasure-city as a girl of thirteen and still did not know where the *Last Supper* was. Caterina knew; she even knew who had made it. "Leonardo da Vinci," she recited proudly. But she had never seen it. She took Viviana away to shop for a trousseau; they bought everything new but shoes, because Viviana was stubborn. She refused to go to the cobbler. *"Ostinata!"* Caterina said, but a certain awe had begun to creep into her fury. Viviana had found an American husband who talked on the radio in New York! Il Duce talked on the radio, too, and they could hear him as far away as America. Viviana a bride! Married, and to a tourist! These were miracles. Someone, Caterina said, had kissed a saint.

The *Last Supper* was deteriorating. It had to be looked at from behind a velvet rope. Viviana said it was a pity the camera hadn't yet been invented when Our Lord walked the earth — a camera would get a *much* better picture of Our Lord than the one in the flaking scene on the wall. Frank Castle taught her how to use his camera, and she snapped him everywhere; they snapped each other. They had settled into Caterina's room, but they had to come and go with caution, so that the manager would not know. It cost them nothing to stay in Caterina's room. Caterina did not say where she went to sleep; she said she had many friends who would share. When Viviana asked her who they were, Caterina laughed. "The priests!" she said. All over the Duomo, Frank Castle was treated with homage, as a person of commercial value. He was an American with an Italian wife. In the morning they had coffee in the dining room. The waiter gave his little bow. Viviana was embarrassed. At the Villa Garibaldi she had deferred to the waiters; no one was so low as the *cameriera*. It made her uncomfortable to be served. Frank Castle told her she was no longer a *cameriera;* soon she would be an American. Unforgiving, she confided that Caterina had gone to stay with the cobbler.

He took her — it was still Nightingale's itinerary — to see the unfinished *Pietà* in a castle with bartizans and old worn bricks; schoolchildren ran in and out of the broad grassy trench that had once been the moat, but Viviana was unmoved. It was true that she admired the luster of Our Lady's lifelike foot, as polished as the marble flagging of the Villa Garibaldi; the rest was mainly rough rock. She thought it ridiculous to keep a thing like that on display. Our Lord didn't have a face. The Virgin didn't have a face. They looked like two ghouls. And this they called religion! What sense was it that the *muratore* who made it was famous — his sprawling Jesus was no more beautiful or *sacro* than a whitewashed wall falling down. And without a face! She let Frank Castle take her picture in her new bird-speckled dress in front of all that rubble, and meanwhile she described the statue of Our Lady that had stood on a shelf in her own plain room at Fumicaro. The Madonna's features were perfect in every detail — there were wonderful tiny eyelashes glued on, made of actual human hair. And all in the nicest brightest colors, the eyes a sweet blue, the cheeks rosy. The Holy Bambino was just as exact. He had a tiny bellybutton with a blue rhinestone in it, to match Our Lady's blue robe, and under his gauzy diaper he even had a lacquered penis that showed through, the color of a human finger, though much tinier. He had tiny celluloid fingernails! A statue like that, Viviana said, is *molto sacro* — she had kneeled before it a thousand times. She had cried penitential floods because of the bleeding that did not come. She had pleaded with Our Lady for intercession with the Holy Bambino, and the Holy Bambino had heard her prayer. She had begged the Holy Bambino, if He could not make the bleeding come, to send a husband, and He had sent a husband.

They walked through rooms of paintings: voluptuous Titians; but Frank Castle was startled only by the solidity of Viviana. Ardor glowed in her. He had arrived in Italy with two little guidebooks, one for Florence and one for Rome, but he had nothing for Milan. Viviana herself was unmapped. Everything was a surprise. He could not tell what lay around the corner. He marveled at what he had done. On Monday, at Fumicaro, Augustine and philosophy; on Thursday, the chattering of a brown-eyed bird-speckled simple-minded girl. His little peasant wife, a waif with a baby inside her! All his life he would feel shame over her. To whom could he show her without humiliation?

Her ignorance moved and elevated him. He thought of Saint Francis rejoicing in the blows and ridicule of a surly innkeeper: *Willingly and for the love of Christ let me endure pains and insults and shame and want, inasmuch as in all other gifts of God we may not glory, since they are not ours but God's.* Frank Castle understood that he would always be mocked because of this girl; he went on snapping his camera at her. How robust she was, how gleaming, how happy! She was more hospitable to God than anyone who hoped to find God in books.

She gave God a home everywhere — in old Roman tubs, in painted wooden dolls: sticks and stones. He saw that no one had taught her to clean her fingernails. He puzzled over it: she was a daughter of a trader in conveniences, she was herself a kind of commodity; she believed herself fated, a vessel for anyone's use. He had married shame. Married! It was what he had done. But he felt no remorse; none. He was exhilarated — to have had the courage for such a humbling!

In front of them, hanging from a crossbar, was a corpse made of oak. It was the size of a real man, and had the head of a real man. It wore a wreath made of real brambles, and there were real holes in its body, with real nails beaten into them.

Viviana dropped to the floor and clasped her hands.

"Viviana, people don't pray here."

Her mouth went on murmuring.

"You don't *do* that in a place like this."

"*Una chiesa,*" she said.

"People don't pray in museums." Then it came to him that she did not know what a museum was. He explained that the pictures and the statues were works of art. And he was married to her! "There aren't any priests here," he said.

She shot him a look partly comical and partly shocked. Even priests have to eat, she protested. The priests were away, having their dinner. Here it was almost exactly like the *chiesa* at Fumicaro, only more crowded. At the other *chiesa,* where they kept the picture of the *Last Supper,* there were also no priests to be seen, and did that prove that it wasn't a *chiesa?* Caterina had always told her how ignorant tourists were. Now she would have to put in an extra prayer for him, so that he could feel more sympathy for the human hunger of priests.

She dipped her head. Frank Castle circled all around the medieval man of wood. Red paint, dry for centuries, spilled from the nail holes. Even the back of the figure had its precision: the draw of the muscles elongated in fatigue. The carver had not stinted anywhere. Yet the face was without a grain of devout inspiration. It was as if the carver had cared only for the carving itself, and not for its symbol. The man on the crossbar was having his live body imitated, and that was all. He was a copy of the carver's neighbor perhaps, or else a cousin. When the carving was finished, the neighbor or cousin stepped down, and together he and the carver hammered in the nails.

The nails. Were they for pity? They made him feel cruel. He reflected on their cruelty — piety with a human corpse at its center, what could that mean? The carver and his model, beating and beating on the nails.

In the streets there were all at once flags, and everywhere big cloth posters of Il Duce flapping on the sides of buildings. Il Duce had a frog's mouth and enormous round Roman eyes. Was it a celebration? He could learn nothing from Viviana. When he asked Caterina, she spat. Some of the streets were miraculously enclosed under a glass dome. People walked and shopped in a greenish undersea twilight. Masses of little tables freckled the indoor sidewalks. Mobs went strolling, all afternoon and all night, with an exuberance that stunned him. All of Milan was calling out under glass. They passed windows packed with umbrellas, gloves, shoes, pastries, silk ties, marzipan. There was the cathedral itself, on a giant platter, made all of white marzipan. He bought a marzipan goose for Viviana, and from a peddler a little Pinocchio on a string. Next to a bookstore, weaving in and out of the sidewalk coffee-drinkers — *"Turista? Turista?"* — boys were handing out leaflets in French and English. Frank Castle took one and read: "Only one of my ancestors interests me: there was a Mussolini in

Venice who killed his wife who had betrayed him. Before fleeing he put two Venetian *scudi* on her chest to pay for her funeral. This is how the people of Romagna are, from whom I descend."

They rode the elevator to the top of the cathedral and walked over the roofs, among hundreds of statues. Behind each figure stood a dozen others. There were saints and martyrs and angels and gryphons and gargoyles and Romans; there were Roman soldiers whose decorated sword handles and buskins sprouted the heads of more Roman soldiers. Viviana peered out through the crenelations at the margins of the different roofs, and again there were hundreds of sculptures; thousands. The statues pullulated. An army of carvers had swarmed through these high stones, century after century, striking shape after amazing shape. Some were reticent, some ecstatic. Some were motionless, some winged. It was a dream of proliferation, of infinity: of figures set austerely inside octagonal cupolas, and each generative flank of every cupola itself lavishly friezed and fructified; of limbs erupting from limbs; of archways efflorescing; of statues spawning statuary. What looked, from the plaza below, like the frothiest lacework or egg-white spume here burst into solidity, weight, shadow and dazzlement: a derangement of plenitude tumbling from a bloated cornucopia.

A huge laughter burst out of Frank Castle's lung. On the hot copper roof he squatted down and laughed.

"What? What?" Viviana said.

"You could be here years and years," he said. "You would never finish! You would have to stay up in the air your whole life!"

"What?" she said. "What I no finish?"

He had pulled out his handkerchief and was pummeling his wet eyes. "If—if—" But he could not get it out.

"What? What? Francesco —"

"If — suppose —" The laughter felt like a strangulation; he coughed out a long constricted breath. "Look," he said, "I can see you falling on your goddamn knees before every *one* of these! Viviana," he said, "it's a *chiesa!* The priests aren't eating dinner! The priests are down below! Under our feet! You could be up here," he said — now he understood exactly what had happened at Fumicaro; he had fixed his penance for life — "a thousand years!"

WHAT HAPPENED
TO THE BABY?

WHEN I WAS A CHILD, I was often taken to meetings of my Uncle Simon's society, the League for a Unified Humanity. These meetings, my mother admitted, were not suitable for a ten-year-old, but what was she to do with me? I could not be left alone at night, and my father, who was a detail man for a pharmaceutical company, was often away from home. He had recently been assigned to the Southwest: we would not see him for weeks at a time. To our ears, places like Arizona and New Mexico might as well have been far-off planets. Yet Uncle Simon, my mother told me proudly, had been to even stranger regions. Sometimes a neighbor would be called in to look after me while my mother went off alone to one of Uncle Simon's meetings. It was important to go, she explained, if only to supply another body. The hall was likely to be half empty. Like all geniuses, Uncle Simon was — "so far," she emphasized — unappreciated.

Uncle Simon was not really my uncle. He was my mother's first cousin, but out of respect, and because he belonged to an older generation, I was made to call him uncle. My mother revered him. "Uncle Simon," she said, "is the smartest man you'll ever know." He was an inventor, though not of mundane things like machines, and it was he who had founded the League for a Unified Humanity. What Uncle Simon had invented, and was apparently still inventing, since it was by nature an infinite task, was a wholly new language, one that could be spoken and understood by everyone alive. He had named it GNU, after the African antelope that sports two curved horns, each one turned toward the other, as if striving to close a circle. He had traveled all over the world, picking up roots and discarding the less common vowels. He had gone to Turkey and China and many countries in South America, where he interviewed Indians and wrote down, in his cryptic homemade notation, the sounds they spoke. In Africa, in a tiny Xhosa village hidden in the wild, he was inspired by observing an actual yellow-horned gnu. And still, with all this elevated foreign experience, he lived, just as we did, in a six-story walkup in the East Bronx, in a neighborhood of small stores, many of them vacant. In the autumn the windows of one of these stores would all at once be shrouded in dense curtains. Gypsies had come to settle in for the winter. My mother said it was the times that had emptied the stores. My father said it was the Depression. I understood it was the Depression that made him work for a firm cruel enough to send him away from my mother and me.

Unlike my mother, my father did not admire Uncle Simon. "That panhandler," he said. "God only knows where he finds these suckers to put the touch on."

"They're cultured Park Avenue people," my mother protested. "They've always felt it a privilege to fund Simon's expeditions."

"Simon's expeditions! If you ask me, in the last fifteen years he's never gotten any farther than down the street to the public library to poke his nose in the *National Geographic*."

"Nobody's asking, and since when are you so interested? Anyhow," my mother said, "it's not Simon who runs after the money, it's *her*."

"Her," I knew, was Uncle Simon's wife, Essie. I was not required to call her aunt.

"She dresses up to beat the band and flatters their heads off," my mother went on. "Well, someone's got to beg, and Simon's not the one for that sort of thing. Who's going to pay for the hall? Not to mention his research."

"Research," my father mocked. "What're you calling research? Collecting old noises in order to scramble them into new noises. Why doesn't he go out and get a regular job? A piece of work, those two — zealots! No, I've got that wrong, he's the zealot, and she's the fawning ignoramus. Those idiot jingles! Not another penny, Ruby, I'm warning you, you're not one of those Park Avenue suckers with money to burn."

"It's only for the annual dues —"

"The League for Scrambling Noises. Ten bucks down the sewer." He put on his brown felt fedora, patted his vest pocket to check for his train ticket, and left us.

"Look how he goes away angry," my mother said, "and all in front of a child. Phyllis dear, you have to understand. Uncle Simon is ahead of his time, and not everyone can recognize that. Daddy doesn't now, but someday he surely will. In the meantime, if we don't want him to come home angry, let's not tell that we've been to a meeting."

Uncle Simon's meetings always began the same way, with Uncle Simon proposing a newly minted syllable, explaining its derivation from two or three alien roots, and the membership calling out their opinions. Mostly these were contentious, and there were loud arguments over whether it was possible for the syllable in question to serve as a verb without a different syllable attached to its tail. Even my mother looked bored during these sessions. She took off her wool gloves and then pulled them on again. The hall was unheated, and my feet in their galoshes were growing numb. All around us a storm of furious fingers holding lit cigarettes stirred up halos of pale smoke, and it seemed to me that these irritable shouting men (they were mostly men) detested Uncle Simon almost as much as my father did. How could Uncle Simon be ahead of his time if even his own League people quarreled with him?

My mother whispered, "You don't have to be upset, dear, it's really all right. It's just their enthusiasm. It's what they have to do to decide, the way scientists do experiments, try and try again. We're sitting right in the middle of Uncle Simon's laboratory. You'll see, in the end they'll all agree."

It struck me that they would never all agree, but after a while the yelling ebbed to a kind of low communal grumbling, the smoke darkened, and the next part of the meeting, the part I liked best (or disliked least) commenced. At the front of the hall, at the side, was a little platform, broad enough to accommodate one person. Two steps led up to it, and Uncle Simon's wife mounted them and positioned herself. "The opera star," my mother said into my ear. Essie was all in yellow silk, with a yellow silk rose at her collarbone, and a yellow silk rose in her graying hair. She had sewn this dress herself, from a tissue-paper pattern bought at Kresge's. She was a short plump flat-nosed woman who sighed often; her blackly gleaming pumps with their thin pedestals made her look, I thought, like Minnie Mouse. Her speaking voice too was mouselike, too soft to carry well, and there was no microphone.

"'Sunshine Beams,'" she announced. "I will first deliver my poem in English, and then I will render it in the lovely idiom of GNU, the future language of all mankind, as translated by Mr. Simon Greenfeld."

It was immediately plain that Essie had designed her gown to reflect her recitation:

Sunshine Beams

> If in your most radiant dreams
> You see the yellow of sunshine beams,
> Then know, O Human Race all,
> That you have heard the call
> Of Humanity Unified.
> So see me wear yellow with pride!
> For it means that the horns of the gnu are
>   meeting at last,
> And the Realm of Unity has come to pass!

"Yellow horn, yellow horn, each one toward his fellow horn" was the refrain, repeated twice.

"The opera star and the poetess," my mother muttered. But then something eerie happened: Essie began to sing, and the words, which even I could tell were silly, were transmuted into reedlike streams of unearthly sounds. I felt shivery all over, and not from the cold. I was not unused to the hubbub of foreign languages: a Greek-speaking family lived across the street, the greengrocer on the corner was Lebanese, and our own building vibrated with Neapolitan and Yiddish exuberances. Yet what we were hearing now was something altogether alien. It had no affinity with anything recognizable. It might just as well have issued from the mouths of mermaids at the bottom of the sea.

"Well?" my mother said. "How beautiful, didn't I tell you? Even when it comes out of *her*."

The song ended in a pastel sheen, like the slow decline of a sunset.

Uncle Simon held up his hand against the applause. His voice was hoarse and high-pitched and ready for battle. "For our next meeting," he said, "the program will feature a GNU rendition, by yours truly, of Shelley's 'To a Skylark,' to be set to music by our own songbird, Esther Rhoda Greenfeld, so please everyone be sure to mark the date . . ."

But the hall was in commotion. A rocking boom was all at once erupting from the mostly empty rear rows, drowning Uncle Simon out. Three men and two women were standing on their chairs and stamping their feet, drumming faster and faster. This was, I knew, no more unexpected than Essie's singing and Uncle Simon's proclamations. It burst out at the close of nearly every meeting, and Uncle Simon reveled in the clamor. These were his enemies and rivals; but no, he had no rivals, my mother informed me afterward, and he took it as a compliment that those invaders, those savages, turned up at all, and that they waited until after Essie had finished. They waited in order to ridicule her, but what was their ridicule if not envy? They were shrieking out some foolish babble, speaking in tongues, pretending a parody of GNU, and when they went off into their customary chanting, wasn't that the truest sign of their defeat, of their envy?

"ZA-men-hof! ZA-men-hof!" Uncle Simon's enemies were howling. They jumped off their seats and ran down the aisle toward the podium, bawling right into Uncle Simon's reddening face.

"Esper-ANto! Esper-ANto! ZA-men-hof!"

"We'd better leave," my mother said, "before things get rough." She hurried me out of the hall without stopping to say goodnight to Uncle Simon. I saw that this would have been impossible anyhow. He had his fists up, and I wondered if his enemies were going to knock him down. He was a small man, and his nearsighted eyes were small and frail behind their fat lenses. Only his ridged black hair looked robust, scalloped like the sand when the tide has run out.

Though I had witnessed this scene many times in my childhood, it was years before I truly fathomed its meaning. By then my father had, according to my mother, "gone native": he had fallen in love with the Southwest and was bringing back hand-woven baskets from New Mexico for my mother's rubber plants, and toy donkeys made of layers of colored crepe paper for me. I was in my late teens when he persuaded my mother to move to Arizona. "Ludicrous," she complained. "I'll be a fish out of water out there. I'll be cut off from everything." She worried especially about what would happen to Uncle Simon, who was now living alone downtown, in a room with an icebox and a two-burner stove hidden behind a curtain. That Essie! A divorce! It was a scandal, and all of it Essie's doing: no one in our family had ever before succumbed to such shame. She had accused Uncle Simon of philandering.

"What a viper that woman is," my mother said. "And all on top of what she did to the baby." She was filling a big steamer trunk with linens and quilts. The pair of creases between her eyebrows tightened. "Who knows how those people out there think — out there I might just as well be a greenhorn straight off the boat. I'd rather die than live in such a place, but Daddy says he's up for a raise if he sticks to the territory."

I had heard about the baby nearly all my life. Uncle Simon and Essie had not always been childless. Their little girl, eleven months old and already walking, had died before I was born. Her name was Henrietta. They had gone to South America on one of Uncle Simon's expeditions — in those days Essie went everywhere with him. "She never used to let him out of her sight," my mother recounted. "She was always jealous. Suspicious. She expected Simon to be no better than she was, that's the truth. You know she was already pregnant at the wedding, so she was grateful to him for marrying her. As well she should be, considering that who could tell whose baby it was anyway, maybe Simon's, maybe not. If you ask me, not. She'd had a boyfriend who had hair just like Simon's, black and wiry. The baby had a headful of black curls. The poor little thing caught one of those diseases they have down there, in Peru or Bolivia, one of those places. Leave it to Essie, would any normal mother drag a baby through a tropical swamp?"

"A swamp?" I asked. "The last time you told about the baby it was a desert."

"Desert or swamp, what's the difference? It was something you don't come down with in the Bronx. The point is Essie killed that child."

I was happy that the move to the Southwest did not include me. I had agitated to attend college locally, chiefly to escape Arizona. My father had paid for a year's tuition at NYU, and also for half the rent of a walkup on Avenue A that I shared with another freshman, Annette Sorenson. The toilet was primitive — it had an old-fashioned pull chain and a crack in the overhead tank that leaked brown sludge. The bathtub was scored with reddish stains that couldn't be scrubbed away, though Annette went at it with steel wool and bleach. She cried nearly every night, not from homesickness but from exasperation. She had come from Briar Basin to NYU, she confided, because it was located in Greenwich Village. ("Briar Basin, Minnesota," she said; she didn't expect me to know that.) She was on the lookout for bohemia, and had most of Edna St. Vincent Millay's verse by heart. She claimed she had discovered exactly which classroom Thomas Wolfe had once taught in. She explored the nearby bars, but legend eluded her. Her yearnings were commonplace in that neighborhood: she wanted to act someday, and in the meantime she intended to inhale the atmosphere. She was blond and large all over. Her shoulder blades were a foot and a half apart and her wrist bones jutted like crab apples. I thought of her as a kind of Valkyrie. She boasted, operatically, that she wasn't a virgin.

I took Annette with me to visit Simon. I had long ago dropped the "Uncle"; I was too old for that. My mother's letters were reminding me not to neglect him. A twenty-dollar bill was sometimes enclosed, meant for delivery to Simon. I knew my father believed the money was for me; now and then he would add an admonitory line. Essie was still living in the old apartment in the Bronx, supporting herself well enough. She had a job in a men's clothing store and sat all day in a back room doing alterations, letting out seams and shortening sleeves. I suspected that Simon was on the dole. It seemed unlikely, after all this time, that he was still being shored up by his Park Avenue idealists.

"Is your uncle some sort of writer?" Annette asked as we climbed the stairs. The wooden steps creaked tunefully; the ancient layers of paint on the banisters were thickly wrinkled. I had told her that Simon was crazy about words. "I mean really crazy," I said.

Simon was sitting at a bridge table lit by a gooseneck lamp. A tower of dictionaries was at his left. A piece of questionable-looking cheese lay in a saucer on his right. In between was a bottle of ink. He was filling his fountain pen.

"My mother sends her love," I said, and handed Simon an

envelope with the twenty-dollar bill folded into a page torn from my Modern History text. Except for a photograph of a zeppelin, it was blank. My father's warning about how not to be robbed in broad daylight was always to keep your cash well swaddled. "Otherwise those Village freaks down there will sure as shooting nab it," he wrote at the bottom of my mother's letter. But I had wrapped the money mostly to postpone Simon's humiliation: maybe, if only for a moment, he would think I was once again bringing him one of my mother's snapshots of cactus and dunes. She had lately acquired a box camera; in order not to be taken for a greenhorn, she was behaving like a tourist. At that time I had not yet recognized that an occasional donation might not humiliate Simon.

He screwed the cap back on the ink bottle and looked Annette over.

"Who's this?"

"My roommate. Annette Sorenson."

"A great big girl, how about that. Viking stock. You may be interested to know that I've included a certain uncommon Scandinavian diphthong in my work. Zamenhof didn't dare. He looked the other way. He didn't have the nerve." Behind his glasses Simon was grinning. "Any friend of my niece Phyllis I intend to like. But never an Esperantist. You're not an Esperantist, are you?"

This, or something like it, was his usual opening. I had by now determined that Essie was right: Simon was a flirt, and something more. He went for the girls. Once he even went for me: he put out a hand and cupped my breast. Then he thought better of it. He had, after all, known me from childhood; he desisted. Or else, since it was January, and anyhow I was wearing a heavy wool overcoat, there wasn't much of interest worth cupping. For my part, I ignored it. I was eighteen, with eyes in my head, beginning to know a thing or two.

I had what you might call an insight. Simon coveted more than the advancement of GNU.

On my mother's instructions I opened his icebox. A rancid smell rushed out. There was a shapeless object green at the edges — the other half of the cheese in his saucer. The milk was sour, so I poured it down the toilet. Simon was all the while busy with his spiel, lecturing Annette on the evil history of Esperanto and its ignominious creator and champion, Dr. Ludwik Lazar Zamenhof, of Bialystok, Poland.

"There they spoke four languages, imagine that! Four lousy languages! And this is what inspires him? Four languages? Did he ever go beyond European roots? Never! The man lived inside a puddle and never stepped out of it. Circumscribed! Small! Narrow!"

"I'll be right back," I called out from the doorway, and went down to the grocery on the corner to replenish Simon's meager larder. I had heard this grandiose history too many times: how Simon alone had ventured into the genuinely universal, how he had roamed far beyond Zamenhof's paltry horizons into the vast tides of human speech, drawing from these a true synthesis, a compact common language unsurpassed in harmony and strength. Yet tragically eclipsed — eclipsed by Zamenhof's disciples, those deluded believers, those adorers of a false messiah! An eye doctor, that charlatan, and look how he blinds all his followers: Germanic roots, Romance roots, Slavic, and then he stops, as if there's no India, no China, no Arabia! No Aleutian Islanders! Why didn't the fellow just stick to the polyglot Yiddish he was born into and let it go at that? Did he ever set foot twenty miles into the Orient, into the Levant? No! Then why didn't he stick to Polish? An eye doctor who couldn't see past his own nose. *Hamlet* in Esperanto, did you ever hear of such chutzpah?

And so on: Esperanto, a fake, a sham, an injustice!

As I was coming up the stairs, carrying bread and milk and eggs in the straw-handled Navajo bag my mother had sent as a present for Simon, I heard Annette say, "But I never knew Esperanto even *existed*," and I saw that Simon had Annette's hand in his. He was circling her little finger with a coarse thumb that curved backward like a twisted spoon. She didn't seem to mind.

"You shouldn't call him crazy," she protested. "He's only disappointed." By then we were already in the street. She looked up at Simon's fourth-floor window. It flashed back at her like a signal: it had caught the late sun. I noticed that she was holding a white square of paper with writing on it.

"What's that?"

"A word he gave me. A brand-new word that no one's ever used before. He wants me to learn it."

"Oh my God," I said.

"It means 'enchanting maiden,' isn't that something?"

"Not if maiden's supposed to be the same as virgin."

"Cut it out, Phyllis, just stop it. He thinks I can help."

"You? How?"

"I could recruit. He says I could get young people interested."

"I'm young people," I said. "I've never been interested, and I've had to listen to Simon's stuff all my life. He bores me silly."

"Well, he told me you take after your father, whatever that means. A prophet is without honor in his own family, that's what he said."

"Simon isn't a prophet, he's a crank."

"I don't care what he is. You don't get to meet someone like that in Minnesota. And he even wears sandals!"

It seemed she had found her bohemian at last. The sandals

were another of my mother's presents. Like the photos of the cactus and the dunes, they were intended as souvenirs of distant Arizona.

After that, though Annette and I ate and slept within inches of each other, an abyss opened between us. There had never been the chance of a friendship. I was serious and diligent, she was not. I attended every class. Annette skipped most of hers. She could spurt instant tears. I was resolutely dry-hearted. Besides, I had my suspicions of people who liked to show off and imagined they could turn into Katharine Cornell, the famous actress. Annette spoke of "thespians" and "theater folk," and began parading in green lipstick and black stockings. But even this wore off after a time. She was starting to take her meals away from our flat. She kept a secret notebook with a mottled cover, bound by a strap connected to a purple sash tied around her waist. I had nothing to say to her, and when in a month or so she told me she had decided to move out ("I need to be with my own crowd," she explained), I was altogether relieved.

I was also troubled. I was afraid to risk another roommate: would my father agree to shouldering the full rent? I put this anxiety in a letter to Arizona; the answer came, unexpectedly, from my father, and not, as usual, in a jagged postscript below my mother's big round slanted Palmer-method penmanship. The extra money, he said, wouldn't be a problem. "Believe it or not," he wrote, "your mother thinks she's a rich woman, she's gone into business! There she was, collecting beaded belts and leather dolls, and God only knows what other cheap junk people like to pick up out here, and before I can look around, she's opened up this dinky little gift shop, and she's got these gullible out-of-staters paying good dollars for what costs your mother less than a dime. Trinkets! To tell the truth, I never knew she had this nonsense in her, and neither did she."

This time it was my mother who supplied the postscript —but I observed it had a later date, and I guessed she had mailed the letter without my father's having seen her addendum. It was a kind of judicial rider: she had put him in the dock. "I don't know why your dad is so surprised," she complained in a tone so familiar that I could almost hear her voice in the sprawl of her handwriting. "I've always had an artistic flair, whether or not it showed, and I don't much appreciate it when your dad puts me down like that, just because he's disillusioned with being stuck out here. He says he's sick and tired of it and misses home, but I don't, and my gallery is already beginning to look like a success, it's all authentic Hopi work! But that's the way your dad is — anywhere there's culture and ambition, he just has to put it down. For years he did it to Simon, and now he's doing it to me. And Phyllis dear, speaking of Simon, he ought to be eating his greens. I hope you're remembering to bring him a salad now and then." A fifty-dollar bill dropped out of the envelope.

That my mother was writing to me without my father's knowledge did not disturb me. It was of a piece with her long-ago attempts to conceal our attendance at Simon's old meetings. But I felt the heat of my guilt: I had neglected Simon, I hadn't looked in on him for ... I hardly knew how many weeks it might have been. Weeks, surely; two months, three? I resented those visits; I resented the responsibility my mother had cursed me with. Simon was worse than a crank and a bore. He was remote from my youth and my life. I thought of him as a bad smell, like his icebox.

But I obediently chopped up lettuce and cucumber and green peppers, and poured a garlic-and-oil dressing over all of it. Then, with the fifty-dollar bill well wrapped in waxed paper and inserted into a folded piece of cardboard with a rubber band around it, I went to see Simon. Two flights below the landing that led to his place I could already hear the commotion vibrating out of it: an incomprehensible clamor, shreds of laughter, and a strangely broken wail that only vaguely passed for a chant. The door was open; I looked in. A mob of acolytes was swarming there — no, not swarming after all: in the tiny square of Simon's parlor, with its sofa-bed in one corner and its makeshift pantry, a pair of wooden crates, in the other, there was hardly a clear foot of space to accommodate a swarming. Yet what I saw through a swaying tangle of elbows and legs had all the buzz and teeming of a hive: a squatting, a slouching, a splaying, a leaning, a curling up, a lying down. And in the center of this fleshy oscillation, gargling forth the syllables of GNU, stood Annette. She stood like a risen tower, solid as bricks. She seemed to be cawing — croaking, crackling, chirring — though in the absence of anything intelligible, how was it possible to tell? Were these the sounds and cadences of the universal tongue? I could not admit surprise: from the start Annette had been so much my unwanted destiny. What else could she be now, having materialized here, in the very bosom of GNU? Or, if she wasn't to be *my* destiny, she intended to be Simon's. She was resurrecting his old meetings — it was plain from the spirit of the thing that this wasn't the first or the last. Anyhow it was flawed. No enemies lurked among these new zealots, if they were zealots at all.

At that time there were faddists of various persuasions proliferating up and down the Village, anarchists who dutifully went home every night to their mother's kitchens, a Hungarian monarchist with his own following, free-verse poets who eschewed capital letters, cultists who sat rapturously for hours in orgone boxes, cloudy Swedenborgians, and all the rest.

These crazes never tempted me; my early exposure to Simon's fanatics had been vaccination enough. As for where Annette had fetched this current crew, I supposed they were picked up from the looser margins of her theater crowd. There were corroboratory instances, here and there, of black stockings and green lipstick. And no Esperantists. Zamenhof was as alien to these recruits as — well, as GNU had been two months ago. Not one of them would have been willing to knock Simon down.

Annette lifted her face from her mottled notebook. All around her the wriggling knots of torsos turned inert and watchful.

"Oh my God, it's Phyllis," she said. "What're you doing here? Can't you see we're in the middle of things, we're *working?*"

"I'm just bringing a green salad for my uncle —"

"Little Green Riding Hood, how sweet. She's not his actual *niece,*" Annette explained to the mob. "She doesn't give a hoot about him. Hey, Phyl, you don't think we'd let a man like that starve? And if you want to know what a real green salad looks like, here's a green salad." She swooped to the floor and swept up a large straw basket (yet another of my mother's souvenirs) heaped with verdant dollars. "This week's dues," she told me.

I surveyed the bodies at my feet, sorting among them. "Where is he?"

"Simon? Not here. Thursday's his day away, but he gave us the new words last time, so we carry on. We do little dialogues, we're getting the hang of it. We're his pioneers," she declaimed: Katharine Cornell to the hilt.

"And then it'll spread all over," a voice called out.

"There, you see?" Annette said. "Some people understand.

Poor Phyl's never figured it out. Simon's going against the Bible, he's an atheist."

"Is that what he tells you?"

"You are *such* a dope," she spat out. "The Tower of Babel's why he got to thinking about GNU in the first place, wasn't it? So that things would go back to the way they were. The way it was before."

"Before what? Before they invented lunatic asylums? Look," I said, "as far as I'm concerned Simon's not exactly right in the head, so I'm supposed to —" But I broke off shamefacedly. "I have to watch out for him, he's sort of my responsibility."

"As far as you're concerned? How far is that? How long's it been since you showed up anyhow?"

Annette, I saw, was shrewder than I could ever hope to be. She was stupid and she was earnest. The stupidity would last, the earnestness might be fleeting, but the combination ignited a volcanic purposefulness: she had succeeded in injecting a bit of living tissue into Simon's desiccated old fossil. She was a first-rate organizer. I wondered how much of that weekly green salad she took away with her. And why not? It was a commission on dues. It was business.

"Where *is* he?" I insisted. I was still holding the bowl of cut vegetables, and all at once discovered a tremor in my hands: from fury, from humiliation.

"He went to visit a family member. That's what he said."

"A family member? There aren't any around here, there's only me."

"He goes every Thursday, I guess to see his wife."

"His ex-wife. He's been divorced for years."

"Well, *he* didn't want that divorce, did he? He's a man who *likes* being affectionate — maybe not to you. He gives back what he's given, that's why, and believe me he doesn't need you to turn up with your smelly old veggies once in a blue moon." Behind her the mob was breaking up. It was distracted, it was annoyed, it was impatient, it was uprooted, it was stretching its limbs. It was growling, and not in the universal tongue. "Just look what you've done," Annette accused, "barging in like that. We were doing so beautifully, and now you've broken the spell."

Circumspectly, I wrote the news to my mother. I had been to Simon's flat, I said, and things were fine. They were boiling away. His old life had nicely recommenced: he had a whole new set of enthusiasts. His work was reaching the next generation; he even had an agent to help him out. I did not tell her that I hadn't in fact *seen* Simon, and I didn't dare hint that he might be courting Essie again: wasn't that what Annette had implied? Nor did I confess that I had unwrapped the fifty-dollar bill and kept it for myself. I had no right to it; it couldn't count as a commission. I had done nothing for Simon. I had failed my mother's charge.

My mother's reply was long in coming. In itself this was odd enough: I had expected an instant happy outcry. With lavish deception I had depicted Simon's triumphant renewal, the future of GNU assured, crowds of mesmerized and scholarly young people streaming to his lectures — several of which, I lied, were held in the Great Hall of Cooper Union, at the very lectern Lincoln himself had once sanctified.

And it was only Annette, it was only the Village revolving on its fickle wheel: soon the mob would be spinning away to the next curiosity.

But my mother was on a wheel of her own. She was whirling on its axle, and Simon was lately at the distant perimeter. Her languorously sweeping Palmer arches were giving way to crabbed speed. She was out of time, she informed me, she had no time, no time at all, it was good to hear that Si-

mon was doing well, after all these years he was finally recovered from that fool Essie, that witch who had always kept
him down, but so much was happening, happening so fast,
the gallery was flooded with all these tourists crazy for crafts,
the place was wild, she was exhausted, she'd had to hire help,
and meanwhile, she said, your father decided to retire, it was
all to the good, she needed him in the gallery, and yes, he had
his little pension, that was all right, never mind that it was
beside the point, there was so much stock and it sold so fast
that she'd had to buy the building next door to store whatever
came in, and what came in went out in a day, and your father,
can you imagine, was keeping the books and calling himself
Comptroller, she didn't care what he called himself, they were
importing like mad, all these kachina dolls from Japan, they
certainly *look* like the real thing, the customers don't know the
difference anyhow . . .

It seemed she was detaching herself from Simon. The
kachinas had freed her. I was not sorry that I had deceived
her; hadn't she taught me how to deceive? For my part, I had
no desire to look after Simon. He was hokum. He was snake
oil. What may have begun as a passion had descended into a
con. Simon's utopia was now no more than a Village whim,
and Annette its volatile priestess. But what had Essie, sewing
her old eyes out in the lint-infested back room of a neighborhood haberdashery, to do with any of it — on Thursdays or
any other day? She had thrown him out, and for reason. I sur-
mised that along with Simon's infidelities she had thrown out
her fidelity to GNU. How many strapping young Annettes
had he cosseted over the decades?

I did not go back to Simon's place. I did what I could to
chuck him out of my thoughts — but there were remind-
ers and impediments. My mother in her galloping prosperity had taken to sending large checks. The money was no lon-

ger for Simon, she assured me; I had satisfied her that he was launched on what, in my telling, was a belated yet flowering career. The money was for me: for tuition and rent and textbooks, of course, but also for new dresses and shoes, for the movies, for treats. With each check — they were coming now in scrappy but frequent maternal rushes — Simon poked a finger in my eye. He invaded, he abraded, he gnawed. I began to see that I would never be rid of him. Annette and her mob would drop him. He would fall from her eagle's claws directly into my unwilling hands. And still I would not go back.

Instead I went down into the subway at Astor Place (where, across a broad stretch of intersection, loomed my lie: the venerable red brick of Cooper Union), and headed for the Bronx and Essie. I found her where time had left her, in apartment 2-C on the second floor of the old walkup. It was not surprising that she did not recognize me. We had last met when I was twelve and a half; emulating my mother, I had been reliably rude.

"You're who?" She peered warily through the peephole. On my side I saw a sad brown eye startled under its drooping hood.

"It's Phyllis," I said. "Ruby and Dan's daughter. From down the block."

"They left the neighborhood years ago. I don't know where they went. Ask somebody else."

"Essie, it's *Phyllis,*" I repeated. "My mother used to take me to hear Uncle Simon."

She let me in then, and at the same time let out the heavy quick familiar sigh I instantly recognized: as if some internal calipers had pinched her lung. She kept her look on me fixedly yet passively, like someone sitting in a movie house, waiting for the horses on the screen to rear up.

"How about that, Simon's cousin's kid," she said. "Your mother never liked me."

"Oh no, I remember how she admired your singing—"

"She admired Simon. She thought he was the cat's pajamas. Like every other female he ever got near, the younger the better. I wouldn't put it past him if he had some girlie in his bed right now, wherever he is."

"But he comes to see you, and he wouldn't if he didn't want to be"—I struggled for the plainest word—"together. Reconciled, I mean. At his age. Now that he's . . . older."

"He comes to see me? Simon?" The horses reared up in her eyes. "Why would he want to do that after all this time?"

I had no answer for this. It was what I had endured an hour or more in the subway to find out. If Simon could be restored to Essie, then—as Annette had pronounced—things would go back to the way they once were. The Tower of Babel had nothing to do with it; it was rather a case of Damocles' sword, Simon's future dangling threateningly over mine. I wanted him back in the Bronx. I wanted him reinstalled in 2-C. I wanted Essie to claim him.

Her rooms had the airless smell of the elderly. They were hugely overfurnished—massive, darkly oiled pieces, china figurines on every surface. A credenza was littered with empty bobbins and crumpled-up tissue paper. An ancient sewing machine with a wrought-iron treadle filled half a wall; the peeling bust of a mannequin was propped against it. In the bedroom a radio was playing; through spasms of static I heard fragments of opera. Though it was a mild Sunday afternoon in early May, all the windows were shut—despite which, squads of flies were licking their feet along the flanks of the sugar bowl. The kitchen table (Essie had led me there) was covered with blue-flowered oilcloth, cracked in places, so that the canvas lining showed through. I waved the flies away. They circled

just below the ceiling for an idling minute, then hurled themselves against the panes like black raindrops. The smell was
the smell of stale changelessness.

Essie persisted, "Simon hasn't been here since never mind
how long it is. Since the divorce. He never comes."

"Not on Thursdays?" The question hung in all its foolishness. "I heard he goes to visit family, so I thought —"

"I'm not Simon's family, not anymore. I told you, I haven't
seen him in years. Where would you get an idea like that?"

"From . . . his assistant. He has an assistant now. A kind of
manager. She sets up his meetings."

"His manager, his assistant, that's what he calls them.
Then he goes out and diddles them. And how come he's still
having those so-called meetings? Who's paying the bills?" She
coughed out a disordered laugh that was half a viscous sigh.
"Those famous Park Avenue moneybags?"

The laugh was too big for her body. Her bones had contracted, leaving useless folds of puckered fallen skin. Her
hands were horribly veined.

"Listen, girlie," she said, "Simon doesn't come, nobody
comes. I do a fitting for a neighbor, I sew up a hem, I put
in a pocket, that's who comes. A bunch of the old Esperantists used to show up, this was when Simon left, but then it
stopped. By now they're probably dead. The whole thing is
dead. It's a wonder Simon isn't dead."

The flies had settled back on the sugar bowl. I stood up to
leave. Nothing could be clearer: there would be no reconcilia-
tion. 2-C would not see Simon again.

But Essie was pulling at my sleeve. "Don't think I don't
know where he goes anyhow. Maybe not Thursdays, who
could figure Thursdays, but every week he goes there. He always goes there, it never stops."

"Where?"

I asked it reluctantly. Was she about to plummet me into a recitation of Simon's history of diddlings? Did she think me an opportune receptacle for an elderly divorcée's sour old grievances?

"Why should I tell you where? What have you got to do with any of it? Simon never told your mother, he never told anyone, so why should I tell *you?* Sit down," she commanded. "You want something to drink? I've got Coca-Cola."

The bottle had been opened long ago. The glass was smudged. I felt myself ensnared by a desolate hospitality. Having got what I came for — or not having got it — I wanted to hear nothing more.

But she had my arm in her grip. "At my time of life I'm not still squatting down there in the back room of somebody's pants store, you understand? I've got my own little business, I do my fittings right here in my own dining room. The point is I'm someone who can make a living. I could always make a living. My God, your mother was gullible! What wouldn't she believe, she swallowed it all."

My mother gullible? She who was at that very hour gulling her tourists into buying Pueblo artifacts factory-made in Japan?

"If you mean she believed in Simon —"

"She believed everything." She released me then, and sank into a deflecting whisper. "She believed what happened to the baby."

So it was not simple grievance that I took from Essie that afternoon. It was broader and deeper and wilder and stranger. And what she was deflecting — what she was repudiating as trivia and trifle, as pettiness and quibble — was Simon and his diddlings. He had his girlies — his assistants, his managers — and for all she cared, staring me down, wasn't I one of them? No, he wouldn't go so far as his cousin's kid, and even if he did, so what? It hardly interested her anyhow that I was his cousin's kid, the offspring of a simple-minded woman, an imbecile who would believe anything, who swallowed it all, a chump for any hocus-pocus . . .

"Ruby had her kid," she said — torpidly, as though reciting an algebraic equation — "she had *you,* and by then what did I have? An empty crib, and then nothing, nothing, empty —"

When I left Essie four hours later, I knew what had happened to the baby. At Astor Place I ascended, parched and hungry, from the subway's dark into the dark of nine o'clock: she had offered me nothing but that stale inch of Coke. Instead she had talked and talked, loud and low, in her mouselike whisper, too often broken into by her big coarse bitter croak of a laugh. It *was* a joke, she assured me, it was a joke and a trick, and now I would know what a gullible woman my mother was, how easy it was to deceive her; how easy it was to trick the whole world. She clutched at me, she made me her muse, she gave me her life. She made me *see,* and why? Because her child was dead and I was not, or because my mother was a gullible woman, or because there were flies in the room? Who could really tell why? I had fallen in on her out of the blue, out of the ether, out of the past (it wasn't *my* past, I hadn't come to be anyone's muse, I had only come to dispose of Simon): I was as good, for giving out her life, as a fly on the wall. And did I want her to sing? She could still sing some stanzas in GNU, she hadn't forgotten how.

I did not ask her to sing. She had hold of me with her fingernails in my flesh, as if I might escape. She drew me back, back, into her young womanhood, when she was newly married to Simon, with Retta already two months in the womb and Simon in his third year at City College, far uptown, dreaming of philology, that funny-sounding snobby stuff (as if a boy from the Bronx could aspire to such goings-on!), unready for marriage and fatherhood, and seriously unwilling. And that was the first of all the jokes, because finally the other boy, the one from Cincinnati who was visiting his aunt (the aunt lived around the corner), and who met Essie in the park every night for a week, went home to Ohio ... She didn't tell Simon about that other boy, the curly-haired boy who pronounced all his *r*'s the midwestern way; even under the wedding canopy Simon had no inkling of the Ohio boy. He believed only that he was behaving as a man should behave who has fathered a child without meaning to. It was the first of all the jokes, the first of all the tricks, but the joke was on herself too, since she was just as much in the dark as anyone: was Retta's papa the Ohio boy, or Simon? Simon had to leave school then, and went to work as a salesman in a men's store on East Tremont Avenue. Essie had introduced him to her boss; she was adept with a needle, and had already been shortening trousers and putting in pleats and letting out waists for half a year.

Their first summer they did what in those days all young couples with new babies did. They fled the burning Bronx sidewalks, they rented a *kochaleyn* in the mountains, in one of those Catskill bungalow colonies populated by musty one-room cottages set side by side, no more than the width of a clothes line between them. Every cottage had its own little stove and icebox and tiny front porch. The mothers and babies spent July and August in the shade of green leaves, among wild tiger lilies as orange as the mountain sunsets, and the fathers came up from the city on weekends, carrying bundles of bread and rolls and oily packets of pastries and smoked whitefish. It was on one of these weekends that Essie decided to tell Simon the joke about the baby, it was so much on her mind, and she thought it would be all right to tell him now because he liked the baby so much, he was mad about Retta, and the truth is the truth, so why not? She had been brought up to tell the truth, even if sometimes the truth is exactly like a joke.

But he did not take it as a joke. He took it as a trick, and for the next two weekends he kept away. Essie, alone with her child and humiliated, went wandering through the countryside, discovering who her neighbors were, and what sort of colony they'd happened into. All the roads were plagued by congregations of wasps, and once the baby, pointing and panting, spied a turtle creeping in the dust. They followed the turtle across the road, and found a community of Trotskyites, beyond which, up the hill, were the Henry George people, and down toward the village a nest of Tolstoyans. Whoever they were, they all had rips in their clothes, they all required mending, they all wanted handmade baby dresses, they all had an eye on styles for the fall, and Essie's summertime business was under way.

When Simon returned, out of sorts, Essie informed him that in the interim she had taken in fifty-four dollars and twenty-five cents, she could get plenty more if only she had a sewing machine, and besides all that, there was a peculiar surprise that might interest him: next door on one side, next door on the other, and all around, behind them and in front of them — why hadn't she noticed it sooner? but she was preoccupied with the baby, and now with the sewing — their neighbors were chattering in a kind of garble. Sometimes it sounded like German, sometimes like Spanish (it never sounded like Yiddish), and sometimes like she didn't know what. Groups of them were gathering on the little porches, which were no more than leaky wooden lean-tos; they seemed to be studying; they were constantly exchanging comments in their weird garble. They even spoke the weird garble to their older children, who rolled their eyes and answered in plain English.

Which was how Simon fell in among the Esperantists. Bella was one of them. She lived four cottages down, and had a little boy a month or two older than Retta. Julius, her husband, turned up only rarely; his job, whatever it was, kept him at work right through the weekend. Bella ordered a dimity blouse and a flowered skirt (dirndl was the fashion) and came often to sit with Essie while she diligently sewed. The two babies, with their pull toys and plush bears, prattled and crowed at their feet. It was a pleasant time altogether, and Simon, when he arrived from the city, seeing the young women sweetly side by side with their children crawling all around them, seemed no longer out of sorts. He was silent now about Essie's deception, if it *was* a deception, because, after all, Essie herself wasn't certain, and the boy from Ohio was by now only a moment's vanished vapor. Besides, Retta's pretty curls were as black and billowy as Simon's own, and Essie was earning money, impressively more than Simon would ever make selling men's underwear in the Bronx. One August afternoon he arranged to have a secondhand sewing machine delivered to the cottage. Essie jumped up and kissed him, she was so pleased; it was as if the sleek metal neck of the sewing machine had restored them to each other.

After that Essie's orders increased, and on Saturday and Sunday mornings, while she worked her treadle, Simon went round to one porch or another, happy in the camaraderie of the Esperantists. They were eager for converts, of course, and he wanted nothing so much as to be converted. Of all of them, Bella was the most advanced. She was not exactly their leader, but she was an expert teacher, and actually had in her possession a letter of praise from Lidia Zamenhof, Zamenhof's own daughter and successor. Bella had sent her a sonnet in fluent Esperanto; Lidia replied that Bella's ingenuity in creating rhyming couplets in the new language remarkably exceeded that of Ludwik Zamenhof himself. There was nothing concerning Esperanto that Bella did not know; she knew, for instance, that the Oomoto religion in Japan held Esperanto to be a sacred language and Zamenhof a god. Zamenhof a god! Simon was entranced; Essie thought he envied Bella even more than he was inspired by her. Also, she felt a little ashamed. It was all those outlandish words Simon loved, he was possessed by them, words had always been his *ambition,* and on account of his wife and the child whose hair was as black and thick as his own he had been compelled to surrender words for a life of shirts and ties, boxer shorts and suspenders.

So when Bella asked Essie to take charge of her little boy for just two hours that evening — perhaps he could be put to bed together with Retta, and Bella would come to fetch him afterward — Essie gladly took the child in her arms, and stroked his warm silky nape, and did the same with Retta, whose nape was every bit as silky, and sang both babies to sleep, while Simon walked with Bella through the grassy dusk to be tutored in the quiet of her porch. An electric cord led indoors; there was a lamp and a table and a bottle of citronella to ward off the mosquitoes and (the point of it all) Bella's weighty collection of Esperanto journals.

It was more than the two hours Bella had promised (it was closer to five, and the crickets had retired into their depth-of-night silence) when she and Simon returned. Simon had under his arm a fat packet of Bella's journals, borrowed to occupy his empty weekday evenings in the city; but it was Bella, not Simon, who explained this. Essie had fallen into a doze in the old stained armchair next to the big bed — Simon and Essie's marital bed — where she had set the babies down, nes-

tled together under one blanket. Retta's crib was too narrow
for the two of them; they lay head to head, their round foreheads nearly touching, breathing like a single organism. Bella
looked down at her sleeping boy, and murmured that it was
a pity to take him out into the cold night air, he was so snug,
why wake him, and could she leave him there until morning?
She would arrive early to carry him off, and in the meantime
wasn't Essie comfortable enough right where she was, in that
nice chair, and Simon wouldn't mind a cushion on the floor,
would he, it would only be for a few more hours . . .

Bella went away, and it was as if she had plotted to keep
Simon from Essie that night. But surely this was a worth-
less imagining: settling into his cushion at Essie's feet, Simon
was fixed with all the power and thirst of his will on Bella's
journals; he intended to study them until he could rival Bella,
he meant to pursue and conquer the language that was to be
humanity's salvation, the structure of it, its strange logic and
beauty, and already tonight, he said, he had made a good beginning — and then, without a sign, in the middle of it all, he
sent out a soft snore, a velvety vibrating hum. Haplessly alert
now, Essie tried not to follow her thoughts. But the night
was long, there was so much left of it, and the mountain chill
crept round her shoulders, and except for the private voice
inside her, a voice that nagged with all its secret confusions,
there was nothing to listen to — only one of the babies turning, and Simon's persistent dim hum. She went on listening,
she wasn't the least bit drowsy, she forced her eyelids shut and
they clicked wide again, of their own accord, like a mechanical doll's. Simon's hum — was it roughening into a wheeze,
or something more brutish than a wheeze? A spiraling unnatural noise; an animal being strangled. But the animal noise
wasn't coming from Simon, it was hurtling out of one of the
babies — a groaning, and then a yowling — good God, was it

Retta? No, no, not Retta, it was Bella's boy! She leaped up to see what was the matter: the child's face was mottled, purple and red, his mouth leaked vomit, he was struggling to breathe . . . She touched his head. It was wildly hot: a tropical touch.

"Simon!"

She pummeled him awake.

"There's something wrong, you have to get down to the village right away, you have to get to the doctor's, the boy's sick —"

"It's the middle of the night, Essie, for God's sake! Bella's coming for the kid first thing, and maybe by then it'll pass —"

"Simon, I'm telling you, he's *sick* —"

In those uncomplicated years none of the *kochaleyns* had a telephone, and few of the families owned cars. On Friday evenings the husbands, Simon among them, made their way up the mountainside from the train station by means of the one ancient village taxi, or else they trudged with their suitcases and their city bundles along the mile of dusty stone-strewn road, between high weedy growths, uphill to the colonies of cottages. The village itself was only a cluster of stores on either side of the train station, and a scattering of old houses inhabited by the year-round people. The doctor was one of these. His office was in his front parlor.

"Go!" Essie cried. Then she thought of the danger to Retta, so close to the feverish child, and seized her and nearly threw her, sobbing, and awakened now by the excitement, into her crib; but the thin little neck under the moistly knotted curls was cool.

"I ought to stop at Bella's, don't you think, and let her know —"

"No, no, don't waste a minute, what's the point, what can she do? Oh listen to him, you've got to hurry, the poor thing can't catch his breath —"

"It's Bella's kid, she'll know what to do," he urged. "It's happened before."

"What makes you think that?"

"Bella told me. She said it in Esperanto actually, when we were working on it last week —"

"Never mind that gibberish, just go and get the doctor!"

Gibberish. She had called the universal language, the language of human salvation, gibberish.

He started down the road to the village: it meant he had to pass Bella's cottage. Her windows were unlit, and he went on. But a few yards beyond her door, he stopped and turned back — how perverse it seemed, how unreasonable, it wasn't right not to tell the mother, and probably the kid would get better anyhow, it was a long walk down the mountain in the dark and cold of the country night, Essie had hurried him out without so much as a sweater, and why wake the poor doctor, a doctor needs his sleep even more than ordinary people, why not hold off till morning, a decent hour, wasn't the main thing to let Bella know?

And here, waiting and waiting, was Essie, with the boy folded in her lap; she kept him there, in the big armchair, lifting him at times (how heavy he was!) to pace from one wall of the narrow room to the other. Now and then she wiped the soles of his feet with a dampened cloth, until he let out a little shudder — almost, it seemed, of satisfaction. But mainly she stood at the window, her wrists aching from the child's weight, watching the sky alter from an opaque square of black to a ghostly pinkish stripe. Retta had long since grown quiet: she lay in the tranquil ruddiness of waxworks sleep, each baby fist resting beside an ear. And finally the white glint of morning struck the windowsill and lit the walls; and at half past eight the doctor came, together with Simon and Bella. He had driven them both up from the village in his Ford. The child was by now perfectly safe, he said, there was nothing the matter that he wouldn't get over, and wasn't the mother told repeatedly not to feed him milk? Her son was clearly allergic to milk, and still she had forgotten, and put some in his pudding.

"You know your boy's had these episodes before," the doctor said, peevishly, "and he may have them again. Because, dear lady, you don't *listen*."

And Bella, apologizing, said, "It's a good thing anyhow we didn't drag you out of your bed at three o'clock in the morning, the way some people would have —"

Essie knew what "some people" meant, but who was "we"?

"While I'm here," the doctor said, "I suppose I ought to have a look at the other one."

"She's fine," Essie said. "She slept through the rest of the night like an angel. Just look, she's still asleep —"

The doctor looked. He shook Retta. He picked up her two fists; they fell back.

"Good God," the doctor said. "This child is dead."

They buried her on the outskirts of a town fifteen miles to the west, in a small nonsectarian cemetery run by an indifferent undertaker who sold them a dog-sized coffin. There was no ceremony; no one came, no one was asked to come. A private burial, a secret burial. In the late afternoon a workman dug out a cavity in the dry soil; down went the box. Simon and Essie stood alone at the graveside and watched as the shovelfuls of earth flew, until the ground was level again. Then they left the *kochaleyn* and for the rest of the summer rented a room not far from the cemetery. Simon went every day to sit beside the grave. At first Essie went with him; but after a while she stayed away. How he wailed, how he hammered and yammered! She could not endure it: too late, that spew, too late, his shame, his remorse, his disgrace: if only he'd gone earlier for the doctor . . . if only he hadn't stopped to see Bella . . . if only he hadn't told her the kid's all right, there's no emergency, my wife exaggerates, morning's time enough to bring the doctor . . . if only he hadn't knocked on Bella's door, if only she hadn't let him in!

In her flat whisper Essie said, "What happened to the baby, maybe it wouldn't have happened —"

She understood that Simon had become Bella's lover that night. She was silent when she saw him carry out Bella's journals and set them afire. The smell of Esperanto burning remained in his clothes for days afterward.

She did not know what the doctor could have done; she knew only that he hadn't been there to do it.

Summer after summer they returned to the town near the cemetery, far from all the *kochaleyns* that were scattered along the pebbly dirt roads in those parts, and settled into the top floor of a frame house owned by a deaf old widower. Simon never went back to his job in the men's store, but Essie kept busy at her sewing machine. She placed a two-line advertisement in the Classified column of the local paper — "Seamstress, Outfits Custom-Made" — and had more orders than ever. Simon no longer sat by the little grave every day; instead, he turned his vigil into a driven penance, consecrating one night each week to mourning. Their first year it was Saturday — it was on a Saturday night that Retta had died. The following year it was Tuesday: Simon had burned Bella's journals on a Tuesday evening. Always, whatever the day and whatever the year and whatever the weather, he walked out into the midnight dark, and lingered there, among the dim headstones, until daybreak. Essie had no use for this self-imposed ritual. It was made up, it was another kind of gibberish out there in the night. She scorned it: what did it mean, this maundering

in the cemetery's rime to talk to the wind? He had deceived
her with Bella, he had allowed Retta to die. Essie never spoke
of Retta; only Simon spoke of her. He remembered her first
steps, he remembered her first words, he remembered how she
had pointed with her tiny forefinger at this and that beast at
the zoo. "Tiger," she said. "Monkey," she said. And when they
came to the yellow-horned gnu, and Simon said "Gnu," Retta,
mistaking it for a cow, blew out an elongated "Moo." And how
Simon and Essie had laughed at that! Retta was dead; Simon
was to blame, he had deceived her with Bella, and what difference now if he despised Bella, if he had made a bonfire of
Bella's journals, if he despised everything that smacked of
Bella, if he despised Esperanto, and condemned it, and called
it delusion and fakery — what difference all of that, if Retta
was dead?

It was not their first summer, but the next, when Simon was
setting aside Tuesdays to visit his shrine ("His shrine," Essie
said bitterly to herself), that he began writing letters to Esperanto clubs all over the city, all over the world — nasty letters, furious letters. "Zamenhof, your false idol! Your god!" he
wrote. "Why don't you join the Oomoto, you fools!"

This was the start of Simon's grand scheme — the letters, the outcries, the feverish heaps of philological papers
and books with queer foreign alphabets on their spines. Yet in
practice it was not grand after all; it was extraordinarily simple to execute. Obscure lives inspire no inquisitiveness. If your
neighbor tells you he was born in Pittsburgh when he was really born in Kalamazoo, who will trouble to search out his
birth certificate? As for solicitous — or prying — relations,
Essie had been motherless since childhood, and her father
had remarried a year after her own marriage to Simon. Together with his new wife he ran a hardware store in Florida;

he and Essie rarely corresponded. Simon himself had been reared in the Home for Jewish Orphans: his only living connection was his cousin Ruby—gullible Ruby, booby Ruby! The two of them, Simon and Essie, were as rootless as dandelion spores. They had to account to no one, and though Simon continued jobless, there was money enough, as long as Essie's treadle purred. She kept it purring: her little summertime business spread to half a dozen towns nearby, and her arrival in May was regularly greeted by a blizzard of orders for the following autumn. She changed her ad to read "Get Set for Winter Warmth in Summer Heat," and had an eye out for the new styles in woolen jackets and coats. She bought, at a discount, discarded pieces of chinchilla and learned to sew fur collars and linings. And all the while Simon was concocting GNU. He named it, he said, in memory of Retta at the zoo; and besides, it announced itself to the ear as New—only see how it superseded and outshone Esperanto, that fake old carcass!

In the fall of each year they moved back to the Bronx. By now Essie owned two sewing machines. "My city Singer and my country Singer," she liked to say, and in the winter worked her treadle as tirelessly as in the summer, while Simon went out proselytizing. He printed up fliers on yellow paper, with long rows of sponsors—lists that were anonymous but for their golden Park Avenue addresses—and tacked them on telephone poles.

It was not surprising, Essie thought, that GNU could attract its earliest adherents—all the *kochaleyns* come home for the winter, and more: the Trotskyites, the Henry George people, the Tolstoyans, the classical music lovers who went to the free concerts at Lewisohn Stadium, the Norman Thomas loyalists, the Yiddish Bundists, the wilder Hebraists, the evolving Thomas Merton mystics, the budding young Taoists and Zen

Buddhists, the aging humanists and atheists, the Ayn Rand enthusiasts . . . and, most dangerously, the angry Esperantists. But after the first few meetings, too many of Simon's would-be converts fell away, the merely inquisitive to begin with, the rest out of boredom, or resentment over dues, or because the rental hall was unheated (the stinginess of those Park Avenue donors!), or because the accustomed messianisms they had arrived with were more beguiling than Simon's ingrown incantations.

"What these people need to keep them interested," Simon argued, "is entertainment. If it's a show they want, Essie, let's give them a show, how about it?"

So Essie was recruited to sing. She had not immediately agreed; the idea of it repelled her, but only until she perceived the use of it; the ruse of it. She was already complicit in Simon's scheme — give your little finger to the devil, and he'll take your whole arm. And even the little finger was not so spare: no matter what Simon's yellow fliers boasted, it was Essie's industry at her two sewing machines that paid for the rental hall. Well then, all right, she'd sing! It turned out, besides, that she had a way with a rhyme. Her rhymes were inconsequential ditties, private mockeries — the latest of her mockeries: the Park Avenue philanthropists were the first of her inventions. As for her singing voice, it had no range, and she was nearly breathless at the close of a long verse, but she poured into it the fury and force of her ridicule, and her ridicule had the sound of conviction. She put herself in the service of Simon's gibberish — why not, why not? Retta was dead, Simon was to blame! Her performances in the cold hall — the costume, the patter, the ditties — were her own contraption, her secret derision, her revenge for what happened to the baby.

And still Simon's meetings shrank and shrank, until only

the quarrelsome diehards remained, and Simon's enemies, the Esperantists.

"Jealousy!" he said. "Because I've outdone them, I've finished them off. And it's Bella who's sending them, it's got to be Bella, who else?"

But it was Essie. She knew where they were, she knew how to find them: she had helped Simon with all those letters calling them fools, she had written their names on the envelopes. Slyly, clandestinely, she summoned them, and they were glad to come, and stand on chairs, and stomp and chant and shriek and pound and threaten. Simon, that usurper, with his shabby homemade mimicry of the real thing, had called them fools! They were pleased to shout him down, and some were even pleased to put up their fists in defense of the sole genuine original universal language, Zamenhof's! Essie herself gave the signal: when she ended those nonsensical couplets, when she hopped off the little podium, the assault began.

She let it go on, winter after winter, with the summer's expeditions to look forward to. From a secondhand bookshop she bought herself a world atlas, and instructed Simon in latitudes and longitudes, all those remote wadis and glaciers and canyons and jungles and steppes he was to explore from May through August (she always with him on every trek, never mind how hazardous), all for the purpose of uncovering fresh syllables to feed and fatten his GNU — while here they sat, the two of them, from May through August, lapping up their suppers of bananas and sour cream at the kitchen counter, half of which held Essie's faithful Singer, on the top floor of the deaf old widower's decaying house.

She let it go on, the meetings winter after winter in the city, in the summers hidden away in their mountain townlet close to Retta's grave. She let it go on until it was enough, until her mockery was slaked, until the warring Esperantists had left him sufficiently bruised to satisfy her. There was more to it than spite, the almost carnal relishing of spite, the gloating pleasure of punishing Simon with his own stick. It was the fantastical stick itself: Essie's trickster apparatus, the hoax of those exotic wanderings, when all the world — simple-minded, credulous world! — believed them to be . . . where? Wherever Dravido-Munda, Bugi, Veps, Brahui, Khowar, Oriya, Ilokano, Mordvinian, Shilha, Jagatai, Tipura, Yurak, and all other teeming tongues, were spoken. From May through August, Essie's atlas marked out these shrewdly distant regions; and on a Tuesday, or a Sunday, or any chosen day of the week, Simon moaned out his gibberish beside Retta's grave in the misty night air.

It did not take long for Annette and her crowd to tire of GNU. They cleared out, I learned afterward, on one of those Thursdays that took Simon conveniently away: there were no goodbyes. When I went to see him again, he was alone. This time, and all the times that followed, I was not prodded by my mother. Her mind was on business; she trusted that Simon was still, as she put it, *blooming*, and I did not disabuse her. She too, she reported, was blooming like mad — it was no longer economical to import the kachinas, so she had gone into producing them on her own. She'd bought up a bit more property, and had a little factory buzzing away, which made not only replicas of the dolls, but all manner of other presumably local artifacts, shawls no Indian had ever worn, moccasins no Indian had ever trod in. Many of these she had designed herself ("I do have this flair," she reminded me), and to tell the truth, they were an improvement on the raw-looking native stuff. My father wrote often, asking when I was coming out for a visit, since from my mother's point of view a trip to New York was out of the question: they had their hands full, the business was so demanding. I answered with com-

monplace undergraduate complaints — I had too many papers overdue, catching up would consume the winter break,
and as for vacation later in the year, I was intending to take
courses all summer long.

I was becoming an easy liar. My papers were not overdue.
I was reluctant to witness my mother's pride in turning out
fakes.

The checks she continued to send (with my father's signature over "Comptroller" in print) grew bigger and bigger. I
cashed them and gave the money to Simon. He took it sadly,
idly, without protest. He was unshaven and wore his sandals on bare feet. His toenails were overgrown and as thick
as oyster shells. His breath was bad; he had an abscess on a
molar that sometimes tormented him and sometimes re-
ceded. I begged him to see a dentist. Little by little I had begun to look after him. I tipped the grocery boy and hired the
janitor to take a brush to the toilet bowl. He had given up
those fruitless hours among alien lexicons; but every Thursday he put on his frayed city hat, with its faded grosgrain ribbon, and locked the door of his flat and did not return until late the next afternoon. I imagined him in a rattling train
headed upstate, toward a forgotten town in the Catskills; I
imagined him kneeling in the dark in damp grass alongside a
small stone marker. I went so far as to conjecture what Thursday might commemorate to a mind as deluded as Simon's:
suppose it was on a Thursday that Essie had confessed her
doubts about the baby; suppose it was on a Thursday that Simon first heard about the curly-haired boy from Cincinnati
— then the grieving guilty mourner at the graveside might
not be a father at all, but only the man Essie had gulled into
marriage long ago. If he did not know which one he was, the
father or the dupe, why should he not be half mad?

And what if everything Essie had confided was a fickle fable, myself (like those flies to her sugar bowl) lured into it, a partner to Simon's delusions?

The sophomore term began. One morning on my way to class I saw, across the street, Annette and two young men. The men were dressed in gray business suits and striped ties and had conventional short haircuts. All three were carrying leather briefcases. Annette herself looked less theatrical than I remembered her, though I could not think why. She wore a silk scarf and sober shoes with sharp little heels.

"Hey, Phyl," she called. "How's your uncle nowadays?"

Unwillingly, I crossed the street.

"Tim. John. My old roommate," she introduced me. Close up, I noticed the absence of lipstick. "Is Simon O.K.? I have to tell you, he changed my life."

"You wrecked his."

"Well, you were right, maybe I took him too seriously. But I got something out of it. I'm in the School of Commerce now. I've switched to accounting, I'm a finance major."

"Just like Katharine Cornell."

"No, really, I have this entrepreneurial streak. I figured it out just from running Simon's meetings."

"Sure, all that green salad," I said, and walked off.

I did not honestly believe that Annette had wrecked Simon's life. It was true that her defection had left him depleted, but some inner deterioration, from a source unknown to me, was gnawing at him. Perhaps it was age: he was turning into a sick old man. The tooth abscess, long neglected, had affected his heart. He suffered from repeated fits of angina and for relief swallowed handfuls of nitroglycerin. He implored me to visit more often; there were no more Thursdays away. I had come to suspect these anyhow — was it conceivable after so many decades that he would still be looking to set his thin haunches on the damp ground of a graveyard, and in snowy winter to boot? Had there been, instead, a once-a-week lover? One of those girlies he diddled? Or Bella, secretly restored? He had no lover now. When he put out a hand to me, it was no longer an attempt to feel for my breast. He hoped for comfort, he wanted to hold on to warmth. The old man's hand that took mine was bloodlessly cold.

I loitered with him through tedious afternoons. I brought him petit fours and tins of fancy tea. While he dozed over his cup, I emptied the leaves out of their gilt canister and filled it with hundred-dollar bills: froth and foam of my mother's fraudulent prosperity. I tried to wake him into alertness: I asked why he had stopped working on GNU.

"I haven't stopped."

"I don't see you *do*ing it —"

"I think about it. It's in my head. But lately . . . well, what good does it do, you can't beat the Esperantists. Zamenhof, that swindler, he had it all sewed up long ago, he cornered the market." He blinked repeatedly; he had acquired a distracting twitch. "Is Ruby getting on all right out there? I remember how she hated to go. You know," he said, "your mother was always steadfast. The only one who was steadfast was my cousin Ruby."

Some weeks after this conversation I went to see Essie; it would be for the last time.

"Simon's dead," I told her.

"Simon? How about that." She took it in with one of her shallow breathy sighs, and all at once blazed up into rage. "Who made the arrangements? Who! Was it you? If he's buried *there*, next to Retta, I swear I'll have him dug up and thrown out!"

"It's all right, my mother took care of it. On the telephone, long distance, from Arizona. He's over in Staten Island, my parents own some plots."

"Ruby took care of it? Well, at least that, *she* doesn't know where Retta is. She thinks it was Timbuktu, what happened to the baby. I've told you and told you, your silly mother never knew a thing—"

The apartment had its familiar smell. I had done what I came for, and was ready to leave. But I noticed, though the mannequin still kept its place against the wall, that the sewing machine was gone.

"I got rid of it. I sold it," she said. "I saved up, I've got plenty. There never was a time when I couldn't make a living, no matter what. Even after the divorce. But people came in those days, it was like a condolence call. I don't suppose anyone's coming now."

I said lamely, "I'm here."

"Ruby's kid, why should I care? I mean the Esperanto people, they're the ones who came. Because they saw I was against Simon. Some of them brought flowers, can you believe it?"

"If you were against him," I said, "why did you go along with everything?"

"I told you why. To get even."

"A funny way of getting even, if you did just what he wanted."

"My God, the apple doesn't fall far from the tree, just like your mother, blind as a bat. You don't think I'd let anybody know my own husband managed to kill off my own child right in my own bed, do you?"

She was all zigzag and contradiction: she had taken revenge on Simon; she had protected him. She was both sword and shield. Was this what an improvisational temperament added up to? I was certain now that no word Essie uttered could be trusted.

She had little more to say about Simon, and there was little more she cared to hear. But before I left she pushed her brownish face, wrinkled as a walnut, into mine, and told me something I have never forgotten.

"Listen," she said, "that goddamn universal language, you want to know what it is? Not Esperanto, and not Simon's gibberish either. I'll tell you, but only if you want to know."

I said I did.

"Everyone uses it," she said. "Everyone, all over the world."

And was that it really, what Essie gave out just then in her mercurial frenzied whisper? Lie, illusion, deception, she said —was that it truly, the universal language we all speak?

CPSIA information can be obtained
at www.ICGtesting.com
Printed in the USA
BVHW032041060719
552764BV00001B/141/P